NORTH

NORTH

Alan Zweibel

ILLUSTRATIONS BY ALEX TIANI

VILLARD BOOKS NEW YORK 1984

TO ROBIN AND ADAM

Library of Congress Cataloging in Publication Data

Zweibel, Alan.
North.

Summary: North, a nine-year-old boy dissatisfied
with his parents, travels around the world in search of
the perfect parents, but all of them seem to have flaws.
[1. Parent and child—Fiction]   I. Title.
PS3576.W36N6   1984   813'.54 [Fic]   84-40177
ISBN 0-394-53826-9

Manufactured in the United States of America
9 8 7 6 5 4 3 2
First Edition

"Honor thy father and thy mother."
—Exodus 20:12

"We're pieces of meat. No matter who you are, the second your ability to produce is not up to what they expect it to be, you're disposable."
—Dave Kingman

"Given a choice, I have to go along with Kingman."
—North

NORTH

CHAPTER

1

North was positive he was having a coronary. Yes, he'd had this feeling before. And yes, they all told him over and over again that nine-year-old boys, as a rule, didn't have heart attacks. But as he sat there at the dinner table, sweat gushing from every pore, his upper body expanding like one of those inner tubes that the Little Rascals were pumping way too much air into, North could do nothing but brace himself for the big bang. For the glorious finish. For that final dramatic moment when the rapids that were coursing through his bloodstream would ultimately overwhelm his most vital organ, causing it to dislodge from its rightful place above the lungs, explode through his chest, and fly across the dining-room table before coming to a pathetic, twitching, sputtering halt in front of his parents, who were calmly eating their fruit cocktail. And why shouldn't it land there? They were the reason he was feeling like this, weren't they? North thought so. And according to Dr. Large, that was all that really mattered.

Dr. Large was the man at the family-counseling center who was helping North and his parents through this very curious time. Yes, eleven times a week they visited him at his big office in the Large Building, where he helped North's folks try to figure

out why their only child (who got along quite nicely with the balance of the human race) suddenly became a candidate for Quincy's table whenever he set his eyes upon them.

And there was really no reason for him to be so repulsed by his folks.

"There's really no reason for him to be so repulsed by you," Dr. Large told North's folks—while their quaking boy lay in an amorphous heap in a corner of the big office. And Dr. Large was right. You see, North's folks were plain folks (short folks, round folks), and, while they were never mistaken for good-looking folks, they were not *that* physically atrocious as to induce cardiac arrest. No. There had to be a deeper reason for North to be reacting like this.

"There has to be a deeper reason for North to be reacting like this," said Dr. Large.

But what?

"Hard to say," said Dr. Large. "But I'm a professional. And, if you want my professional opinion, I'd say that North is crying for help."

"So how can we help?" North's parents wanted to know. And who could blame them? No parent wants to see his child cry—especially for help.

"First of all, it's important that you know that deep down North loves you very much." North's parents were very happy to hear this. They felt like skipping.

"Second of all, there's no reason to skip," said Dr. Large. "A loving smile will do just fine. It will tell North that you will always be there for him."

A professional opinion! And since North's folks were concerned folks (suburban folks, nonprofessional folks), they did exactly what Dr. Large prescribed. They smiled. Lovingly. All the time.

So, back at the dinner table, it was just those loving smiles that North found himself staring into as he clutched his breast in a last-ditch attempt to keep his revved-up heart inside of his person. No, those loving smiles *didn't* help. If anything, they became just another gripe on the already long list of gripes that North had against his folks. Think about it. Here he was on the brink of being demoted to the past tense, and his very own mother and father did nothing but sit there smiling. Smiling and eating fruit cocktail. Talk about adding insult to injury! But at this particular moment North was in no condition to talk about anything, insult *or* injury. As a matter of fact, as his body involuntarily stiffened, keeled off his chair, and started flopping around on the dining-room floor like a mackerel out of water, all North was able to say (with what he was quite certain was his last breath) was "This is no way to live."

Yes, North was having a bad time with his folks, and it was putting a damper on what was, in all other respects, a very successful life.

Look at the year he'd had!

> School: 91 Academic Average
> Little League: .402 Batting Average
> Fourth-Grade Musical: "North's Tevye moved me."
> —Kenny Tuchman (Mrs. Benson's class)

A great year? Yes! But did North feel that his parents appreciated his greatness? No! And it drove him nuts!

As smart as North was, he could never figure out why his own parents didn't regard him with the same enthusiasm that the other parents did. It didn't make sense. But it was true. It was only in *other* homes that North was exalted as a model son, the kind of son who sets the standard against which all other sons are compared.

"Why can't you be like North?"

"North helps his mother."

"North can read lips."

"North flosses."

"North pruned the oak."

"Why can't you be like North?"

Quite a boy, huh? But here's the *truly* amazing part. Ordinarily, when one child is compared unfavorably with another child, the first child would like nothing more than to see two Dobermans grab the arms of, and have a tug-of-war with, the child that he's been unfavorably compared with. This is human nature, and it's a universal kid feeling that exists all over the world (except in Venice, where jealous kids much prefer that gondoliers beat them to an unrecognizable pulp with their oars). But such was not the case with North. Not at all. What sense did it make? None. So whenever they were confronted by these comparisons, the only thing that any of the kids ever did was throw their arms up and answer the question "Why can't you be like North?" by saying, *"Nolo contendere."*

A NOTE TO THE READER:

There's no concrete proof that *all* the kids answered the question with this Latin phrase, which means "no contest." Considering that these were all nine-year-old boys, it is probably safe to assume that some of them offered different responses to the question. The important thing to keep in mind, though, is that no matter what Latin, Greek, or foreign expression they *did* answer with, all of them basically said the same thing—that their pal North was a special guy and even to attempt a defense of their own shortcomings was futile and essentially a waste of everyone's time.

What a tribute! What a kid! North's folks were sitting on a gold mine! They really were.

But did they go outside every night and thank their lucky stars for giving them a son who was a star in his *own* right? No! Did they ask the gardener to reshape the hedges into evergreen icons of this heroic lad? No! And did they hire a voice coach to teach them how to sing a hymn that praises *him*? Are you kidding? North was lucky if he made it through dinner in one piece.

Dinner at North's house was not a pretty picture. Mom and Dad sat at opposite ends of the table, and words flew back and forth between them like bullets at the Alamo. Not bad words, mind you. Oh no. North's folks never said bad things to each other. Only good things—about themselves.

Mom: forever gabbing about a new hair color or about some diminishing species that she saved from being clubbed into extinction because she collected a few nickels.

And Dad: #6. That's all he spoke about, as if he were a broken record. #6, #6, #6 . . .

A NOTE TO ANY READER
WHO'S WEARING NEW PANTS
Look inside your pocket. Is there a tag that says "Inspected by #6"? That's North's Dad!

A grim vision indeed. According to these two, the entire continent would be without baby seals and we'd all be walking around with deformed trousers if it weren't for them.

And North? Well, about three weeks before, he thought he had a shot at getting in a word edgewise. He really did. All during dinner he sat there trying his utmost to contain the excitement that was welling up inside of him. Great news (it was about the science fair)! But North knew that timing was the key. Absolutely. The only way he even had a prayer of being heard was if his timing was perfect. So, like a deer at a road crossing, North stood on the edge of their conversation, rocking patiently and waiting for his chance to dash between the heavy flow of self-praising adjectives and first-personal pronouns to tell them about the blue ribbon he got for his project . . . Now?

"Hey, remember that weather vane I made for the sci—"

"—so, there was no way in hell that *I* would ever give corduroys like that *my* approval . . ."

Dad. Something about belt loops. North retreated.

To keep his mind off the mounting frustration that was starting to bloat his entire being, North let his mind wander and thought about a contest he wanted to promote. A race. That's right—a foot race. Two contestants: light vs. the speeding sound of stupidity. Winner take all. Only one stipulation, though. It had to take place right here at the dinner table.

". . . and I told the girls on the committee that if every agnostic in Calcutta would send just one cow to Biafra, UNICEF could start concentrating on some other country for a change."

Mom. Light didn't stand a chance in this room. And neither did North, unless—and North knew this was a long shot—unless Moses just happened to burst into the house and lead the children of Israel over Mom's and Dad's mouths so they'd shut up and let North tell his great news about the science fair. Otherwise . . .

Then, it happened. North was summoned back to the reality of dessert by the deafening lull in his folks' conversation. Was this his opportunity to speak? Now? But how could he be sure? He'd been fooled in the past. Now! Bulging with anticipation, North looked both ways before he spoke. To the left—Mom was committing her sherbet to her lips. To the right— Dad's spoon was already in his mouth. Now!

"Hey, remember that weather vane I made for the sci—"

North never knew what hit him.

You know, when you consider the fact that he had partaken of close to 3,200 desserts with these people, it's hard to believe that North could've fallen for an ambush—but that's exactly what happened. You see, North miscalculated just how far along Dad was with his spoonful of sherbet because, just as North was reaching full stride with his science announcement, Dad licked his lips and proclaimed: "I saw some blood in my stool this morning."

A sucker punch that straightened North right up and sent him reeling. It made him dizzy. The room and everything in it started to spin. Then Mom moved in for the kill. Not to be outdone by her spouse's solil- oquy on proctological probes and over-the-counter softeners, Mom devoured her sherbet much quicker than the frozen delight was ever intended to be con- sumed. And (somehow enduring the discomfort that the sudden introduction of cold dessert inflicts upon the eyes and certain passages in one's sinus region) Mom proceeded to recount every stroke that she and every other woman took that afternoon at the Subur- ban Women's Daily Afternoon Golf Classic.

North was staggering—kept upright only by virtue of the verbal crossfire that he was caught between. But his defenses were completely down, and he no longer had the strength to hold back the stream of headlines that were relentlessly snaking their way through his body. Yes, the floodgates were open. A raging flow of involuntary secretions carrying the suppressed news about the blue ribbon, countless other blue ribbons, high grades, grand-slam home runs, curtain calls, and merit badges created an inner turbulence whose momentum was irreversible. He was going to get their attention!

But due to years of conditioning, North's involuntary secretions knew better than to head for North's mouth. No, they'd been frustrated far too often in the past. So, once they got as far as the uvula, North's secretions faked right, went left, and buttonhooked back toward his chest.

Hence, North's first cardiac event. And hence:

"North!"

"Are you okay?"

"North!"

North couldn't believe it. He really couldn't. After landing on the table (he'd grazed the chandelier!), he actually heard the voices of Mom and Dad saying:

"North!"

"Oh, my God!"

"North!"

They were saying *his* name in a context that had nothing to do with *them*. They were paying attention to *him*. And a week later, when North had his next attack, they also paid attention. And three days after that they paid attention. And the next time, and the next . . .

With each passing day, it took less and less provocation on the part of North's folks to trigger their lad's newest reflex—the situation degenerating to the point where now, three weeks after his first attack, the mere sight of their faces gave North's central nervous system carte blanche to let all hell break loose.

At first, North didn't mind having to be near death to get his folks to acknowledge his life. He really didn't. Hey, the end justified the means. But then, Dr.

Large. And then, those smiles. And now? Well, North was now beginning to feel just a little silly. And who could blame him? A boy can take just so much cardio-vascular abuse from his folks before he comes to the conclusion that they may not be worth it anymore.

So North became depressed. You see, he felt that life is short enough as it is. And while there were many goals which he had set out to accomplish for himself during his allotted time on Earth, getting snuffed out before his age reached double digits was definitely not one of them.

No, something had to be done about this.

CHAPTER

2

North had a secret spot. Now, to most people, this spot wouldn't seem like anything special. But to North it was a place where he could go and do his best thinking. A place where he could sit for hours and hours and change the world into the way he wanted it to be.

It's really hard to say when an ordinary spot is discovered to have something special about it. And if you'd asked North himself, he too would've been hard put to pinpoint the exact moment and the exact circumstances under which this spot revealed its special

powers to him. What he did know was that on this spot, and on this spot only, whatever he wanted to see, he saw. And whatever he wanted to be, he was. It was all so simple from his secret spot. All he had to do was sit down in that large, black, cushiony armchair, lean back in a reclining position, concentrate, and that was it. The secret spot did the rest. And the fact that this was all done in full view of whoever happened to be walking around in the furniture department of the department store where the armchair was located didn't matter at all to North. Why should it? No one had any way of knowing what he was up to. As far as they were concerned, this was just another little boy who had fallen asleep in an armchair waiting for his parents to finish shopping. And as far as North was concerned, this only helped to make his secret spot that much more of a secret.

And if North ever needed the refuge of this secret spot, it was the very next day. Twelve hit batters! Unbelievable! One dozen straight Panthers granted free passage around the bases, compliments of North's fusillade. That a display like this could be put on by last season's most valuable pitcher was a source of astonishment to teammates and fans alike. Could a nine-year-old lose his stuff that quickly? "Probably not," said Mr. Blank, the team's coach. "But something does seem to be bothering him."

How perceptive! It was true—for the first time ever, North let something in his personal life affect his performance on the field. So after the game, while local buffs went scurrying to the record books to compare his dubious achievement against what was already entered, North left the ball field and headed straight for his secret spot.

North, still in uniform, sat there patiently. He knew
from experience that closing one's eyes and waiting
for specific pictures was a slow, evolving process—not
unlike the way that the primitive television set down-
stairs in his parents' basement used to take a long time
to warm up before it flickered into view. So he waited.

And sure enough, it came. Slowly, but it came. At
first a vague, blurry vision that lazily began to contract
into focus: the tennis shoes, the jogging outfit, the
designer-framed eyeglasses, the Sony Walkman . . . it
was Mom! (For a second, North thought it would've
made more sense if the eyeglasses were the first thing
to appear, as if the introduction of this prescription
were the reason that he could see the other features
more clearly. Not a bad thought! But then he remembered that Mom was blind as a bat and that bats were
rodents, so North made a mental note never to have
that thought again.)

Then Mom's image became reduced and moved to
the left half of North's vision, making room for another
pair of tennis shoes, a jogging outfit, designer-framed
eyeglasses, a Sony Walkman . . . Dad!

Mom and Dad. Dad and Mom. As if he were looking
at mug shots down at the station house, North saw
his folks: in profile, head-on, and in profile again.
Mom and Dad. Dad and Mom. Home-movie symbols
of love, security, and happy times:

> Dad in the chef's hat . . . the Lincoln Memorial . . .
> North on a pony . . . Mom in the Chesapeake . . .
> Grandpa's sixty-fifth . . .

What memories! And there were more:

> Oversleeping in Scranton . . . the time they wore those
> costumes . . . washing the Gremlin . . . the day they

returned the encyclopedias . . . Grandpa's sixty-seventh . . .

Happy times? Yes. Times when Mom and Dad could do no wrong and were exempt from objective evaluation.

But memories were *past* times—and it was current and future times that North was now concerned with. So, turning his attention back to the mug shots, North saw different images as he fast-forwarded his life to the present:

> The bathroom sink after Dad shaved . . . the sounds Mom made when she chewed gum . . . Dad sticking his pinky into his ear and shaking it real fast . . .

When had it happened? At what point did the traits that North had always considered to be accepted parental privileges lose their special status and begin to make him dubious about the people who practiced them?

> Mom eating one pea at a time . . . Dad in a restaurant, scratching his back with a fork . . . Mom putting Saran Wrap around her legs before exercising . . . Dad having himself paged at the World Series . . . Mom not knowing who Magellan was . . . Dad always trying to say the phrase "Having my baby" while he was burping . . .

These were the people *North* was trying to please? The people who didn't appreciate *him*? The people whom he was allowing to (figuratively *and* literally) break his heart? Just who did they think they were? It was a small wonder he had lasted *this* long.

No! No more! Sure, deep down he *may* have loved

his folks; but right now he didn't feel it. No, right now he was mad. Mad that he had let things get *this* far. And mad enough that he wanted to make sure that it would never happen again. Yes, North wanted to be happy. But if he couldn't be happy with his folks, whom could he be happy with?

North opened his eyes and looked at the procession of shoppers and browsers as they tended to their business of shopping and browsing. People. Lots of people. Some by themselves, some with each other. Moms. Dads. Potential Moms and Dads?

North leaned forward in his secret spot, as if to get a better look at how he saw himself with some of *these* folks. Like those folks who were comparing the stereos (musical folks, dancing folks). North thought he'd look great with them. And he also was sure he'd look great with the folks who were buying the hot tub (clean folks, aquatic folks).

North found himself starting to get excited about looking great. He really did. But he wasn't the impulsive type. No, he needed more information. So he got up off his chair and approached a very pregnant lady who was looking at a crib.

"That's a nice crib," said North. And it was!

"Thank you. And you're a nice boy."

North bowed at the waist.

"Ma'am?"

"Yes?"

"May I ask you a personal question about your unborn child?"

"Sure."

"Will you love him?"

"I already do."

"But he's not even alive yet."

"Yes, he is. Life begins at conception."

North didn't feel like debating.

"But will you be proud of him?"

"Absolutely. Especially if he's a kind person with a good heart."

North couldn't agree more.

A man in the sporting goods department was pounding his fist into a brand-new baseball glove. North, still in uniform, spoke first.

"You need oil to soften the leather on that mitt."

"Oh, I'm not buying it," said the man.

"How come?"

"My playing days are over."

"What about your son?"

The man shook his head. "I have four girls."

"Do you love them?" North wanted to know. He had to know.

"Very much. But I'd still give anything to have a boy —to play ball with."

"Anything?"

"You bet."

"How about a boy who batted .402 last season?" (North didn't think it was necessary to tell him about those twelve pelted Panthers.)

".402?" The man smiled. "Now that would certainly be a bonus, wouldn't it?"

A bonus!

"You mean like a real late bedtime, and iced tea after a tough game, and a cost-of-living increase in his weekly allowance?"

The man smiled again and went back to pounding the glove. But he didn't say no!

North's confidence was growing. He swaggered up to a man and woman who looked very sad.

"Would having a son cheer you up?"

The man looked at him.

"You're North, aren't you?"

"Yes, I am he."

"So why do you tease us like this?"

"Excuse me?"

"Everybody knows my wife is barren."

North was sorry to hear this. He stopped swaggering. "I'm not teasing you. Would you like a son like me?"

"Who wouldn't? God knows I'd sleep a lot better knowing that a son like you would be heir to my shipbuilding business . . ."

All of a sudden, North started spinning. Three, four, five times he spun around, in place, and then ran back to his secret spot, way before the sad businessman ever had a chance to complete his sentence. There was so much to think about (and, while it was not like North to be rude, he always did his best thinking when he wasn't spinning).

So he retook his seat, closed his eyes, and thought about it. All of it. Unconditional love! Astronomical allowances! Shipbuilding! Fun thoughts. And before too long, while sitting there in his uniform, North first gave thought to the prospect of becoming a free agent.

CHAPTER

3

"You can't expect me to sit on a story like this. What a scoop!" Winchell, eight and a half, was ecstatic. North had just told him his idea of becoming a free agent. About going around the country and offering his services as a devoted son to the highest-bidding set of parents.

"Hey, Winchell, I told you this stuff because you're my best friend. Not because you're editor of the school newspaper."

"I'm a journalist, North."

"So?"

"So you never said that this conversation was off-the-record."

"Winchell . . ."

A NOTE TO THE READER WHO DOESN'T
TRUST WINCHELL:
Pick up Winchell. Okay, now throw him. Measure the distance. That's how far he should be trusted.

"This could be my Watergate!"

"Winchell, I came to you for advice."

"Advice?"

"Yeah. Advice."

"Well, my advice is to do it now—while you're still hot."

"But I need time to think . . ."

"North, a few more games like that Panther game and some of the more attractive parents might start to have second thoughts . . ."

That damn Panther game!

". . . and, North, that arithmetic test we took today?"

"What about it?"

Winchell lifted the top of his school desk, reached in, and pulled out a Xeroxed copy of North's arithmetic test.

"You got a 59."

"Where did you get that test?"

"I'm a journalist, North. I can't reveal my sources. Besides, how I got this test is not important"—Winchell pointed to the red 59 as well as to the teacher's comment, "How could this be?" to emphasize his point—"but why you got this grade *is* what's important."

"I know."

"So there's nothing to think about. Unless . . ."

"Unless what?"

"Unless you don't have the guts to go through with it."

North stood toe to toe with Winchell and looked him straight in the eye when he responded.

"Winchell, I'm nine years old. I watch a lot of old movies on TV. Do you really think I'm going to fall for a line like that?"

It was a rhetorical question. Winchell knew that. That's why he didn't answer it.

"I just feel that I owe it to my parents to tell them what my plans are. I don't want them to hear about it from anybody else."

"Still the good boy, huh, North?"

"Maybe."

"I see. But that leaves you with one problem."

"What's that?"

"I got a newspaper to get out."

"Winchell . . ."

Winchell looked into the eyes of his friend North. In one eye, he saw his best pal making a simple, reasonable request for time. In the other eye, he saw himself accepting a Pulitzer.

"Winchell . . ."

"Oh, I'm sorry. What did you say your name was again?"

"You're going to burn me, aren't you, Winchell?"

Another rhetorical question. But Winchell chose to answer this one.

> We interrupt our program to bring you a special news bulletin.

Back at his secret spot, North couldn't help but be stunned by what was going on in front of him. Not that there's a conventional way of informing one's folks that they are about to become former folks (ex-folks, forsaken folks), mind you. It's just that, given the choice, he still would've preferred that his intentions be conveyed on a more personal note than by having a newscaster hold up a special edition of the school newspaper, whose headline read:

"I'm Outta Here"
—North

Can you imagine sitting in a department store and seeing yourself on television? Can you imagine seeing yourself on forty televisions? Ordinarily North enjoyed watching television in the department store because he liked to play this little game where he'd look at one set and then quickly look at another set to see if the same exact thing was happening at the same exact time or if maybe there was a slight delay and he'd be quick enough to see the same thing happening again. Yes, it was a great little game. But as North's eyes made their appointed rounds from screen to screen, the game came to a screeching halt the moment North saw the smiling man who was standing there, in person, between two of the televisions. The smiling man? Yes, he looked familiar. But where did he come from? Where did North *know him* from? And why was he looking at North and doing a commercial right there in the store?

"Thinking of dropping your folks like a sack of hot potatoes? Well, maybe we could help."

Wait a second . . . That smile. That voice. That sports jacket. Could it be? Could it possibly be?

"Hi. I'm Arthur Belt."

It was! It was Arthur Belt! From that famed law firm of Jacobie and Belt! That's where North recognized the smiling man from. From all of those great TV commercials where he told you another of his forty-seven reasons why you should use Jacobie and Belt.

"Reason #48 . . ."

They'd added another reason!

"Boy, is this case going to cause a commotion!"

And boy, was Arthur Belt right. The news about North spread like wildfire and everyone immediately took sides. No casual observers here. Oh, no. The

issue of childhood free agency was far too sensitive for anyone not to get excited, one way or another, about it. And, almost predictably so, public opinion was polarized along generational lines, with the kids siding with North and the folks throwing their support behind North's folks.

"What a great idea," said a kid.

"It's absurd," said a folk.

HONK IF YOU HATE NORTH said a bumper sticker.

"North's folks framed Oswald" became the Cub Scout motto.

Yes, North had touched a nerve. He was challenging the lords of domestic hierarchy, and while all the kids marveled at his gumption, none of the folks were going to take his threat to their power lying down. No way. Except for two folks, that is. North's folks. They took the whole thing lying down. Literally. Hey, they were under sedation, so what other posture could they possibly assume? Slight lean forward, right leg bent, and arms outstretched like the winged messenger in those tele-florist commercials?

Hardly. Look, just to keep things in their proper

perspective: If Mr. Ed himself had been shot up with as many sleep inducers as Dr. Large had injected into them, the talking horse would only have had time to say "Good night, Wilbur" before crashing to the floor of his paddock.

No, North's folks were not taking the prospect of their lad's defection very well at all. Although in retrospect one could argue that they were indeed fortunate to have been in Dr. Large's office when they received the bad news. As a matter of fact, it was upon returning from the lavatory (a copy of Winchell's special edition tucked neatly under his arm) that Dr. Large carved his name into the annals of bedside manner when he sat them down, held their hands, and did his best to soften the blow.

"Knock knock," said Dr. Large.

"Who's there?" asked North's folks.

"Your boy."

"Your boy who?"

"Your boy who will soon be somebody else's boy."

Perhaps it was his delivery. Did he telegraph the punchline? Or maybe he should have warmed up North's folks by opening with a song. But really, who's to say why any given piece of comedy material, as hysterical as it may be, can vary as to how it's appreciated by different audiences? "Hysterical" is an interesting word. It could mean very funny, or it could mean having the color drain from your face, having your eyes journey into the recesses of your forehead, howling like a carnival barker, and then wantonly destroying an analyst's office furniture—which really *isn't* very funny. Well, North's folks opted for that second definition. Hence, the call to 911. Hence, those injections in the back of the siren-screaming ambulance. And hence, their semiprivate room at the Even Larger Medical Center.

Hours before the store opened, a naked North stepped onto the escalator and made his way up toward the Linen Department. Yes, he should've grabbed a towel *before* he showered in the Stall-Shower Department. And yes, this was the first time that he'd ever been naked on a moving escalator. But then again, this was also the first time he'd ever actually lived in a department store—so new experiences such as these were to be expected.

Because his folks' home was now a stomping ground for the press, autograph seekers, sketch artists, tourists, and just about anyone who happened to be *anyone's* child, North had no choice but to hide out. And what better way to escape the curious throng than to take up residence in the department store where his secret spot was located? And it was working out great. Sure, there were still a few wrinkles that had to be dealt with; but for the most part, North was adapting quite nicely to his new "home"—sleeping in the George Washington Slept Here Bed Department, doing his homework in the Ethan Allen Revolutionary War Rolltop Desk Department, finding diversion in the Video Village Video Games Department, and enjoying late-night cheese in the Pretentious Shoppers Gourmet Shoppe. It was the perfect store for North to live in while he was in guardian limbo, and no one even noticed that this media giant was habitating in their midst. How could they? Not with all the excitement about the upcoming Fourth of July White Sale.

Yes, the Fourth of July. North kept thinking about that particular date as he got dressed in the Boys Who Are Almost Young Men's Clothing Department. Independence Day. Talk about symbolism! But it was possible. According to Arthur Belt, North could very well be a free agent by the time our nation's birthday rolled around. Pretty quick work, considering that it was only a few days ago that North had made his emancipation proclamation. But then again, why should anyone expect anything but the fastest results and the most effective legal action when one's best interests were in the hands of as eminent an attorney as Arthur Belt?

"No. There will be no trial by jury," Arthur Belt told the press.

"Could you explain why, sir?" a reporter shouted.

"Of course I can. You see, North is the plaintiff. Which means that in a jury trial, his folks would be judged by their peers. And who are North's folks' peers? Other folks. And everyone knows how *they* feel about this case. My client wouldn't stand a chance."

"But what if the jury was twelve sedated folks?" the same reporter shouted.

Arthur Belt shook his head. "That'd be even worse," he explained. "A jury like that could be in deliberation until North is well into his thirties. What's the sense?"

"So who *is* going to try this case?" shouted the reporter.

Arthur Belt couldn't take it anymore. "You know, if there were a crowded press conference with dozens of reporters fighting to be heard, I could understand your shouting, Winchell. But during lunch where it's just the two of us—"

"I'm sorry."

"—in a booth in a diner, it seems sort of silly. *Especially* when I'm trying to leak secret information to you."

"I said I was sorry."

Arthur Belt hesitated just long enough to give the

impression that he wasn't going to forgive Winchell. Then:

"Okay, you're forgiven."

Though he was no relation to Arthur Belt, Judge Buckle was forever indebted to North's barrister. After all, it *was* Arthur Belt who had saved Judge Buckle's life in Korea. Wasn't it?

The time: 1951.

The place: a tent somewhere along the 38th parallel.

The situation: Pvt. Belt's cleaning his rifle; the weapon accidentally goes off; the bullet finds a home to the right of Buck Pvt. Buckle's left nipple.

Yes, a lesser man might have panicked. But like all men of true grit, Arthur Belt took what had all the earmarks of a negative experience and made it work *for* him—by sprinting to headquarters, stealing the chaplain's Bible, inscribing "To my dear friend, Judge" on the inside cover, purposely firing another round that went through the pages of the Holy Book, racing back to the tent where the fallen Buckle lay bleeding, strapping the Scriptures to Judge's chest, and then convincing him that the pages of the Testament had cushioned the impact of the enemy's bullet and had most probably saved his life.

What a tale! And now, here they were, two old war buddies, sipping tea in Judge Buckle's chambers, located on the third floor of the Stately Paneled Chambers Building, and reminiscing about the past. The good old days? And even today, the very sight of Arthur Belt brought Judge Buckle to the brink of tears.

"You know, what bothers me the most about that incident is that I don't remember your ever giving me that Bible."

"Judge, there was a war going on. We were preserving democracy. Who had time for thank-you notes?"

"It's still not like me, though." Judge Buckle dabbed the corner of his eye with the hem of his robe.

"Forget it, Judge."

"I'm sorry, Arthur."

"Okay, you're forgiven."

"Thanks, Arthur. Now what can I do for you?"

"Well, it's the North case."

"Oh, yes. I just read that I'm judging that one."

"And that's why I'm here. I'm North's attorney."

"Oh, Arthur . . ."

This time Judge Buckle gave in to his emotions and allowed himself the tears that he was fighting so desperately to hold back. The irony of it all: two war buddies who had shared a tent along the 38th parallel, reunited thirty-three years later to determine the destiny of a boy who's nine. Judge Buckle knew, he just knew, that those numbers were symbolic of *something*. And because of that, he started crying like a baby judge.

"Oh, Arthur . . ."

"Hear me out," said Arthur Belt. "Because what I have to say is important."

"I'm sorry."

Arthur Belt hesitated just long enough to give the impression that he, too, was choked up with emotion. Then:

"We go back a long way, Judge."

"I know . . ."

"But what transpired between us should not affect your impartiality in this case . . ."

"I know . . ."

". . . because even though I just so happened to salvage your very existence, I feel it would be a grave miscarriage of justice for personal sentiment to bias your decision."

"I know . . ."

Judge Buckle was now wailing like a banshee. But Arthur Belt forged ahead.

"So our eternal bond aside, I want you to promise me that you are going to be fair to both parties involved and base your judgment solely on the facts."

"You're amazing, old buddy."

"I believe in truth, Judge Buckle. Do I have your word?"

"Yes."

"Promise?"

And before Judge Buckle even had a chance to answer the same question a second time, North's attorney's hand disappeared into the inside pocket of his plaid sports jacket and then reappeared clutching a pocket-size Bible that had a bullet-size hole running through it.

And just before Judge Buckle lost all control of those devices that differentiate human beings from quivering mounds of Jell-O, he placed his right hand on the holey book and yelled, "I swear."

CHAPTER

4

There was no way that North could possibly oversleep—not with all the alarm clocks in the Alarming, Yet Digital, Grandfather Clock Department set to go off at the same time. Sure, it would've been easier to set just one clock for the time he wished to awaken. But since today was going to be such an important day (and with snooze alarms being what they are), North couldn't risk the chance of oversnoozing, as it were. So at precisely 8:40 on the Thursday morning that Judge Buckle was to hear the case of *North* vs. *North's Folks*, every buzzer, bell, AM station, FM station, chime, tone, and *bing-bong* imaginable blended into one cacophonous wake-up blare that even the dead would have had little choice but to respond to.

After turning off all the clocks, North dressed in the clothes that he'd laid out on a chair (his secret spot!) the night before. North had never worn a three-piece suit before, and choosing this particular herringbone outfit was something he had given a lot of thought to. The way he figured it, if all those bad guys he saw on the news wore good clothes when their cases came up, shouldn't this "lad for all seasons" at least do the same when *he* went to court? After all, who wants to be dressed worse than a felon? Not North. Not today. Not in front of all those people who were out there rallying when North's bus pulled up in front of the Order in the Court Building.

Everyone was there! Kids, folks, cops, the press, bands, whites, blacks, and even people who had *more* than one syllable. Like vendors. Vendors who sold posters, T-shirts, buttons, streamers, candy, whistles, decals, banners, and items that had as many as *three* syllables. Like confetti. And all those mentioned above were voicing their feelings by displaying, shaking, wearing, twirling, throwing, and hurling all those items mentioned above.

Yes, they all expressed their feelings. And so did North. After he was safely escorted inside, he began to feel that anxious feeling that nine-year-olds usually feel in anticipation of seeing their folks for the first time after having spent an entire week in a department store. But once again, it was Arthur Belt to the rescue.

"It's not as if they're not going to be compensated," North's attorney reasoned. "You see, according to the plan I've proposed, you are a major minor."

"What does that mean, Mr. Belt?"

"Well, it means that you are under age, which makes you a minor, right?"

"Right."

"However, since you've spent nine consecutive years with the same folks, that gives you the right to accept or reject the offers made by other folks. Which means you won't end up being reared by anyone you don't like—ever again."

"And what about my folks—my natural folks, I mean?"

"They have the right to be compensated with either another kid or something else that's nine years old."

"That sounds fair. I guess."

"Oh, it's going to be great."

"That's if I win," said North, with just a slight hint of reasonable doubt in his voice.

"North," scolded Arthur Belt with the unflagging confidence that only a man who had graduated from a foreign law school would ever dare to have.

"I'm sorry."

"Okay, you're forgiven."

"Let me remind everyone that this is not a trial," Judge Buckle reminded everyone. "This is a hearing. Both sides are going to say things and I am going to hear them. No doubt all of you will hear the same things that I am hearing. This is your privilege. However, once both sides have been heard, it will then be my turn to pass judgment. Obviously, all of you can pass judgment, but it won't count. That's my privilege because I'm the one who's the judge. Have I made myself clear to the plaintiff?"

Arthur Belt stood up, then looked at North sitting next to him ever so obediently, before declaring, "Yes, it is quite clear to the plaintiff."

"And is it clear to the defense?" asked Judge Buckle.

Dr. Large stood up, then looked down at North's still-sedated folks, who were asleep in the cots that a bailiff had helped carry into the chambers, before declaring, "Your Honor, the defense rests."

"I've heard enough," said Judge Buckle. "In my judgment, any folks who would sleep through a hearing like this are irresponsible folks. Therefore, I have no choice but to rule in favor of the plaintiff."

Unbelievable! Nine years of indentured childhood

and now, liberty! After a judicial hearing that took only twelve seconds.

The system worked!

North was free!

CHAPTER

5

The North free-agency draft took place a week later, and rumors ran amok about which folks North would wind up with. Some insisted that he'd end up with West Coast folks, while Las Vegas oddsmakers said the smart money was on Motown. Despite the speculation, North opted to keep a low profile and spent the day on his secret spot while Arthur Belt fielded the calls from folks who wanted a fair shot at the boy who, as one writer put it, "could turn any family around."

The rules were simple. Any set of folks could draft North by calling, toll-free, 1-800-ART-BELT. After that the folks were to submit a financial statement and medical records, and write a composition entitled, "Why I Deserve to Pick Up Where North's Parents Left Off."

A NOTE TO THE READER:
Blind folks were allowed to submit cassettes.

Then, those folks who survived the first cut were asked to please be patient, as they would soon be informed when North would be coming to spend some time with them. Arthur Belt thought it wise to limit the list to no more than nine sets of folks.

"Everyone wants a piece of you and that's good," explained Arthur Belt. "But the fewer sets of folks that you audition, the more serious they'll each think you are about them."

"So?"

"So that will give them more incentive to prove themselves worthy."

"Oh."

"Plus the fact I don't want the calendar to become a factor."

"What does that mean?"

"That means that I'd like you to spend as much time as you need evaluating each set of parents, but I would also like to see you settled with a family by Labor Day, so you could start the new school year in your new hometown."

What a summer! Two full months of traveling and being romanced and trying to figure out who would be the best to help you become whoever you decide to be. What a welcome change this was for a boy whose previous summer was highlighted only by the lulls between cardiac upheavals. Yes, this was going to be great. So great that North closed his eyes, leaned back, and savored what he realized could very well be his last few moments on this particular secret spot.

CHAPTER
6

North had never been in an airplane before, so it was understandable why he had so many questions about the dynamics of flight.

"Excuse me, stewardess."

"Yes, North?"

"How fast is this jet going?"

"We're cruising at a speed of 535 miles per hour."

"Then can I ask you a question?"

"Why, of course."

"Well, if I stand in the aisle and I jump up and just sort of hang there in midair—"

"If anybody could do it, it's you."

"—would the plane pass under me, causing my body to splatter against the back wall of the economy section?"

A great question! But North was just getting started.

"Excuse me, Captain Cody?"

"Hello, North. Welcome to the cockpit."

"Captain Cody, can I ask you a question about the black box that the flight recorder is in?"

"Sure. What about it?"

"Well, since that box is hardly ever destroyed when there's a crash, why don't they just build big black planes out of the same material?"

"What a great question!" said Captain Cody.

"It *would* make things safer," said Co-Captain Co-Cody.

"What a great question!" said the whole crew in unison.

Yes, North's mind was really working the way he always knew it could if he was given the chance to be optimistic. And boy, was North ever optimistic! Right now his spirits were as high as the 747 that was carrying him toward his formative years.

First stop:

"New Mom? New Dad?"

"Howdy!" yelled the Texas folks.

Yes! The Texas folks. As North stepped off the plane, he knew, he just knew, that the folks with those big hats were the Texas folks. Sure, everyone in the terminal was wearing a really big hat. But when North saw the folks who were standing amidst all those prized cattle that had (N) branded on their hides, he just knew that those Texas folks were *the* Texas folks.

"Let us take a look at you," requested the Texas folks. Fair enough. After all, they *did* pay for his flight. North nodded, then posed.

"My, he looks smaller than in his pictures," observed Ma Tex. But Pa Tex didn't seem to be as concerned as his marital sidekick.

"Ah, no reason to fret. We'll beefen him up," he predicted with a laugh so hearty that the cattle started to sway.

"C'mon, son," beckoned Pa Tex. "There's lots to talk about."

"But I have to claim my baggage first."

"Nonsense."

"But all my clothes—"

"We have all new clothes for you, son."

"Cowboy clothes?"

"You're darn tootin'. Cowboy boots and cowboy shirts and cowboy hats—"

"Spurs? For my boots?"

"Of course. Not to mention—"

"A long little doggie? An old man called 'Gramps'?"

"Son, we got everything."

The Texas folks! Not only did they have everything, but everything they had was big: the car that took them home from the airport, the bar that was in the car that took them home from the airport, as well as the bartender who tended the bar in the car that took them home from the airport. Everything was huge!

"Thirsty, son?" asked Pa Tex.

Although North wasn't driving (and legally wouldn't be allowed to do so for another eight years), he still thought it best to remain sober. Folks, he figured, should be chosen with a clear head.

"Anything soft?"

"Anything *soft?*" Pa Tex repeated with a laugh so hearty that the bartender started to do the hokey pokey. "What an understatement!" And with that, Pa Tex rolled down his window and pointed.

"See that Orange Crush bottling plant?"

"Sure."

"It's yours, son."

"Excuse me, Pa Tex?"

"That *is* your favorite soda pop, isn't it?"

"Yes—"

"We also know that you enjoy a hot bowl of pastina every now and then."

"Yes, I do."

"We've done our homework, son," said Ma Tex. "Everything there is to know about you, we now know. And, we like what we've learned! That's why we're so willing to give you anything you want, to make you happy as our son."

The car turned into the driveway. Three hours later, it pulled up in front of the Texas folks' house.

"It's all yours. Name it," said Pa Tex. "The main house, the guest house, the livestock . . ."

"Tell him about the oil," pleaded Ma Tex.

"I was just getting to that. Son, we have oil."

"Crude?" North asked, although he hadn't the foggiest notion what that meant.

"The crudest," bragged Pa Tex. "The crudest, blackest, lumpiest, oiliest oil you ever did see."

"That's good." North still didn't know what he was saying.

"It's the best! Everything I own is the biggest 'n' the best, 'n' that's why I want you to be my boy, because you're the best—"

"Thank you."

"—'n' before too long, you'll also be the biggest."

"Excuse me?"

"We'll explain everything to you after dinner." Ma and Pa Tex showed North into the dining room, which had a buffet fit for an entire rugby team.

"Is company coming?" asked North.

"What a sense of humor," beamed Ma Tex.

"We gotta remember that one," roared Pa Tex.

"Come on, son. Grab yourself a couple of hams,

some sides of beef, a few dozen potatoes, 'n' sit down 'n' eat."

Dinner took forever. Hey, how couldn't it?

"Have some more pies for dessert, son."

"No! I mean, 'No, thank you,' Ma and Pa Tex."

"Full?"

"I'm stuffed."

"Ah, don't worry," said Pa Tex. "Before too long you'll see that your stomach will stretch 'n' stretch 'n' your capacity for food will grow 'n' grow."

Pa Tex said this as if this were a terrific thing to have happen to your stomach.

"And then you'll be like Buck." Ma Tex smiled.

"Who?"

"Buck *was* big, wasn't he," Pa Tex said as a statement, as opposed to a question.

"The biggest," Ma Tex reassured him nonetheless.

"Who?"

"Our first son. Buck. He was the biggest boy in Texas," explained Ma Tex. North was afraid to ask the next question. But he just had to.

"He *was* the biggest boy?"

"Buck died."

"Oh, I'm so sorry, Ma and Pa Tex. How did he die?"

"The biggest stampede in history," said Pa Tex.

"Oh . . ."

"He must've been trampled by every horse in Texas," added Ma Tex.

"Oh . . ."

North came *this* close to quipping that Buck was now perhaps the *flattest* boy in Texas but something, just something, told North that this was neither the time nor the place for such levity. No, it was quite apparent to North that these Texas folks were deeply saddened by what had happened to their son, and North was respectful of their grief. However, he still

didn't understand what all of this Buck business had
to do with him.

"When we lost our Buck, we were devastated," said
Pa Tex. "He was everything to us. And because he
was such a special lad, we felt that no one could ever
replace him in any way, shape, or form. And then, we
read about you. Your talents, your achievements, your
leadership qualities, as well as your basic bone structure, have given us new hope that we can once again
be blessed with a boy who has the potential to grow
into someone we can be proud of and show off to the
world on all fifty-seven local TV stations that we own
and operate. Please think about it," urged the Texas
folks.

And that's exactly what North did. He thought
about it that very evening as he climbed, rung after
rung, up the twelve-foot ladder that extended from the
floor to the mattress of what was once Buck's bed. And
he gave it even more thought as he swung from the
rope in an attempt to shut off what was once Buck's
reading lamp.

North's thoughts? This was a tough one. Oh, sure,
he thought it would be great to finally be appreciated
the way that one so unique *should* be appreciated.
That was everything that North desired. And these
Texas folks did seem to have the desire, as well as the
means, to make a special kid feel that he *was* special.

A   NOTE   TO   THE   READER   WHO   FEELS   A
''BUT''   COMING   ON:
Here it comes.

But, as appealing as all this seemed, there was
something about this Texas situation that bothered

North. You see, in his heart of hearts, North really didn't know why he should forever be compared with, and live in the shadow of, someone who had died in a stampede. What kind of life would that be? What kind of *shadow* would that be? Well, if the dimensions of the furniture in Buck's bedroom were to be taken seriously, odds were that it could very well be a shadow that North would never be out of.

North knew that this was going to be one of those decisions that were so hard to make, but once made, left you feeling that much better. What a predicament! He really did like these Texas folks, and he really didn't want to let them down, but . . . No! He had to be honest with himself. He couldn't do it. He couldn't settle at this point. Hey, why live in Texas if you're not really going to be the only star in this, the Lone Star State? Plus, if he came this close to finding a suitable set of folks at this, the first leg of his quest, he could barely imagine what might still be waiting out there for him. Yes, North finally made his decision and he *did* feel better.

So early next morning, after taking the scaffold down the side of what was once Buck's toilet, a much relieved North got dressed, sang "Happy Trails" to the Texas folks, was driven to the airport, and then waited there for twelve hours so he could fly off into the sunset.

It was only a matter of time until North's plane flew out of the sunset and landed on an aircraft carrier. Yes, this leg of his journey *was* to audition the Hawaiian folks, but how would this patriotic lad ever be able to forgive himself if he didn't make a quick stop at Pearl Harbor to pay his respects?

"If only you had been here that morning," said Admiral Bass as he escorted North past all the seamen who, in their dress whites, were standing at attention. "It could've made all the difference if we'd had you." Since the Day of Infamy had taken place well over thirty years before he was born, North *had* to be flattered by the admiral's little game of make believe.

"A kid like you . . . No way they ever would've caught *you* by surprise."

Maybe so. But what did surprise North was the cadets. Because, though they were still in formation, it was obvious that they were not "at ease"—shuffling about, shifting their weight from one foot to the other.

"They're getting antsy," said Admiral Bass, who then stopped walking and made a personal appeal to North. "Look, would it be too much to ask, I mean, I know you must be tired from your flight but . . ."

"Say no more, Admiral. You know I'd do anything to entertain our armed forces." And with that, North dropped to the ship's deck, and immediately reeled off scores of perfect military push-ups. So perfect, in fact, that these military men actually broke formation and started cheering and throwing their hats up in the air, just as they do when they win the Army-Navy football game.

"Thank you," said Admiral Bass. "Thank you very much."

Later that evening, his personal USO performance behind him, North, after a relaxing seafood dinner at the captain's table, stood at the ship's bow and looked out at the ocean. The Pacific. An exciting new body of water that North hoped was leading him to an exciting new set of folks. Sure he was disappointed by what had happened in Texas. But if North was going to be mature about this whole venture, he knew he would have to expect *and accept* that any set of folks (no matter how good their credentials looked on paper) might still have a shortcoming or two. Plus, there was certainly no need to panic at this point. Not at all. If anything, just the mere thought of spending the balance of his childhood in a place like Hawaii was starting to make North more tropically enthusiastic than most nine-year-olds ordinarily become.

Hawaii. Yes! Sun, surf, sand, *Five-O* types of adventure. Hawaii. Our fiftieth (and probably most important) state. Why *else* would Hawaii be in that special box in the lower left-hand corner of maps of the United States if there weren't something great about it?

Yes, Hawaii did sound exciting. But North wasn't going to let himself get *too* excited. Not just now, anyway. No, North thought it best to maintain his composure while he was still in view of all those cadets who were still jumping and cheering and celebrating over his push-ups. The way North figured it, *somebody* on this ship had to keep a cool head. So just in case (God forbid) there was another sneak attack, North was ready.

But genuine enthusiasm is a hard thing for anyone to contain. It really is. So when the ship came to port and the admiral threw a Hula-Hoop around a mooring to secure things, an ecstatic North bolted onto the dock and rushed to meet the Hawaiian folks.

The Hawaiian folks were fine folks (tan folks, Don Ho's folks), and they recognized their potential boy-to-be the moment they saw him.

"Hi, North."

"Hi, North."

"Hi, Ho. Hi, Ho."

> **A NOTE TO THE READER:**
> North came *this* close to singing "It's Off to Work We Go," but he stopped himself because he didn't want them to think he wanted to go off and work—because he didn't.

Yes, their greeting was cheerful enough, but something about their limp handshakes told another story. North didn't respect limp handshakes. No, North was a firm believer in the firm handshake. To him it was a sign of strength, conviction, and self-esteem. It was a way of saying to the world, "Hey, I'm alive. So look at me because I'm here on this earth and I demand to be heard." The Hawaiian folks? Well, theirs was more like, "Excuse me for breathing, but my backbone's a Slinky." But why? Why the tentative handshakes?

There's something happening here . . . and what it is ain't exactly clear, North thought to himself. But whatever it was, it bothered him. How couldn't it? Because as far as he was concerned, people who shook hands like that usually had—in addition to their wrist, forearm, and elbow—something *else* up their sleeves.

First impressions aside, it was during the ride in the motorcade that North started to become acquainted with the Hawaiian folks. Poppa Ho had a great job (he was governor!), which gave Momma Ho the right to stand next to him on almost all occasions. And, aside from his elected position as head of this potentially volcanic state, Poppa Ho was a major stockholder in a soap company (Lava!), so he and Momma Ho had the luxury of having something to fall back on, should they ever lose their status as Hawaii's first folks.

It all sounded so attractive—and not only the material things. Oh, no. The fact that if North settled here he would be so many hours younger (because of the difference in time zones) had its own appeal. Hey, it was *all* appealing except . . . those handshakes. For the life of him, North just couldn't shake those handshakes.

The Getting-to-Know-North luau took place on the beach behind the Hos' house, and everyone who lived in Hawaii was there. What a bash! Hawaiian food, shirts, punch—as well as a huge rectangular structure that North had trouble identifying because it was covered with a big white sheet. It just stood there, in the corner of the beach along the water's edge, and to North it looked like a wrinkled drive-in movie screen. Could it be? Hey, it made perfect sense to North that drive-in movies would be even more popular here than back home because the sun rises in the east and sets in the west, and since Hawaii was so far west, it should get extraordinarily dark, better to enjoy movies outdoors.

"Are we going to see a picture, Poppa Ho?"

"Wait and see," said a beaming Poppa Ho. "Wait and see, you little rascal, you."

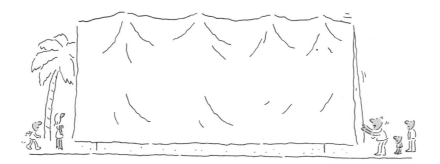

Those handshakes, those handshakes. And it wasn't only *the* Hawaiian folks who shook hands like that. No. Everyone North was introduced to extended a dead fish, and it was beginning to drive North nuts!

It was right after dessert (Baked Alaska!) that Momma and Poppa Ho strode to the side of the huge sheet-covered structure and asked for everyone's attention.

"Ladies and gentlemen, this is a great day. And there're going to be a lot more great days because Mrs. Ho and I have decided that we're going to outbid anyone, anywhere, and do whatever it takes to make North Hawaii's first son."

Applause.

"Not only will this satisfy us on a personal level, but let's be honest—if people see that North chose us over everyone else, well, I think it will solve all of our emotional problems."

Louder applause.

"Because, as far as I'm concerned, I can't think of any better advertisement for our state than . . ."

And on that cue, Poppa Ho tugged on a long rope that allowed the big white sheet to drop to the white sandy ground, unveiling the gigantic billboard that said:

Pandemonium! Yes! Everyone at the luau simply
went nuts—cheering, singing, snorkling, and con-
gratulating one another with *firm* handshakes. And
North? Well, he too was excited. But in a slightly different way.

"What is *that?*" he shouted at Poppa Ho, while
pointing to his likeness on the billboard.

"Son, it will be in every airport, along every high-
way, and on every TV commercial in every city in—"

"My crack?"

"Your what?"

"My crack. You mean to tell me . . ."

"Son . . ."

". . . that my crack . . ."

"Son . . ."

". . . is going to be seen by . . ."

"Uh, son . . ."

"What gives you . . ."

"Oh, son . . ."

". . . the right . . ."

"Hey, son—"

". . . to show my—?"

Although North was undeniably a specimen in
every way, there were certain parts of his physical
being that he was quite modest about. And his crack,
well, his crack certainly fell into that category.

"Now look, son," said Poppa Ho. "There's no other
way."

"No other way to what?"

It was then that both of the Hawaiian folks felt to
their knees and started crying.

"Why do you think we're so insecure? Why do you
think our handshakes are so tentative?"

Those handshakes . . . those handshakes.

"I'm speaking for *all* of Hawaii now. We feel used.
People come here on their vacations—all pale and

tired from their long flights—they eat, they swim, and they walk around telling one another that it's a nice place to visit, but they'd go out of their minds if they had to live here. So one week, or maybe ten days later, they leave. Now I ask you, how would you like that? What would that do to your self-image? For goodness' sake, we don't even have a self-image. Quick, tell me, are Hawaiians Polynesians, or are Polynesians Hawaiians, or are we not at all related and it's just an amazing coincidence that we look exactly like one another?"

As smart as he was, this was the first time in recent memory that North was stumped for an answer to any question. And it was also, to his recollection, the first time that he'd every prayed for a tidal wave, or Diamond Head, or *any* natural disaster to bail him out of a conversation. Poppa Ho was really starting to pour it on.

"But if you lived in Hawaii, people would be more inclined to settle here and—"

"—and you'd feel that much better about yourselves," said North, finishing the whinin' Hawaiian's sentence for him.

"Precisely."

Again North had a decision to make. And though it wasn't as difficult as the one he had had to make in Texas, spoiling a luau that is being held in your honor is never an easy thing for anyone to do. But what choice did North have? Here he was, looking for a worthy set of folks, and these people were looking for North to validate *their* existence? No. There was something very wrong about that.

"Would you like to go hang gliding, son?"

There was also something very wrong with the hang glider. It was paisley. And North would never allow himself to be caught *dead* flying around in a paisley hang glider.

"You're going to leave us, aren't you?"

It was true. North's mind was made up.

"You're just like the rest of them."

North resented that. He always resented it when he was compared with other people. But once again, North showed his individuality—by not waiting a week or ten days to leave the island. No, he only stayed as long as it took to bow at the waist, say "Thank you for a very lovely Getting-to-Know-North luau," and bid goodbye to the Aloha State.

The nerve of those Hawaiian folks! Expecting North to shoulder the responsibility for *their* happiness. Wasn't he already responsible for the glee and merriment of one generation? His generation.

Yes, millions of kids had made the verdict of "The Great White North Decision" work to their advantage and, as a result, were having the best summer of their lives. Allowances had soared, bedtimes were a forgotten practice of the past and the folks had little say in the matter. How could they? If any folk even entertained the notion of discipline or any traditional form of parental authority, the kids laughed in their faces and threatened to "Go North" if their folks didn't behave.

Emotional blackmail? Absolutely. Folks were being bilked for everything they were worth. But it was working. All one had to do was drive through any community and see Dads mowing lawns, taking out garbage, walking dogs, weeding gardens—performing any household chores that the kids *used* to do— while the kids themselves sat in lounge chairs barking commands like:

"And after you clean my room, I want you to run to the store and buy me three more bicycles."

"Yes, son."

While Moms, relegated to around-the-clock dessert-making, would serve the fruits of their labor to their offspring:

"Mom?"

"Yes?"

"In the next batch, I'd like the eclairs to have a lot more custard in them."

"Whatever you say, son."

"And, Mom?"

"Yes?"

"Could you please do me a favor?"

"Anything you want, son."

"From now on, could you please curtsy after you serve me."

"Yes, son. I'm sorry, son."

Yes, the kids were flexing their muscles. But they hadn't forgotten how this position of power had come about. Oh, no. That's exactly why whenever an unreasonable demand was made and whenever an outlandish request was honored, it became second nature for the kid who was getting his own way to bow his head and whisper the words "*Viva El Norte.*"

A NOTE TO THE READER:

Once again, there is no way of knowing how many kids actually said this phrase, which, loosely translated, means "Long Live North." However, it's probably a good guess that the kids who said the words "*Viva El Norte*" were the same kids who earlier had said, "*Nolo contendere.*" As for the other kids? Well, they were also very grateful to North.

NORTH TO ALASKA

Although North's plane landed safely, it didn't stop spinning for close to two days. Hey, this was the Arctic, and it was just as North had always imagined it. That's right—North flew in to spend some time with the Eskimo folks, and the runway was icy. Hence the forty-eight-hour skid that finally came to a halt when the pilot unfastened his seat belt and lassoed it around the North (no relation) Pole.

And the Yukon made perfect sense at this point in North's itinerary. It really did. After the letdown he'd suffered in the paradiselike setting of Hawaii, he needed an emotional lift. He needed a change of scenery. He needed to be away from crowds. He needed time to think. Hey, let's face it—North needed the sub-zero temperatures, the barren wastelands, and the howling windchill factors that the Arctic had to offer.

Yes, the Arctic folks. The Arctic folks were igloo folks (frigid folks, tundra folks), and when they met North, they greeted him with a frozen daiquiri.

"Thank you, Poppa Chill, but I don't drink," said North.

"Iced tea?" offered Momma.

Yes!

The sleigh ride from the airport was uneventful—no fanfare, no pomp, no commotion—and North welcomed this change.

"We are not flashy folks," said Poppa Chill between shouts of "Mush" to the pulling huskies. "You see, even though we live at the top of the world, we're really very down-to-earth people."

"Work. That's all we do," added Momma. "We work the land. We fish. We hunt. Eskimo folks have no time to be posh folks."

"Pride. That's what motivates us," said Poppa Chill. "But we need something in our lives that we can take pride in, aside from our work. And that's where you come in."

Yes!

"I'm a very rich man," said Poppa Chill. They were home now, sitting around the hole in the kitchen floor, fishing for snacks. "You see, a few years ago, the government gave us a lot of money to move out of our old house because the Pipeline was going to be built through our living room. I accepted their offer and now I am wealthy." Something was nibbling on North's line. It was a baby seal. But fret not. No species could ever be endangered when with the ecologically sensitive North. He threw it back. "Now all that money, North—it's yours. Take it."

Yes!

"You can speak to your accountant about the best way to shelter this money, but I really wouldn't worry too much about taxes because Eskimos don't pay any."

"They don't?"

"Well, we should. But the IRS considers it a hassle to come all the way up here and audit—so they just take our word about things."

The honor system. Yes! Yes!

And just what did the Arctic folks want from North!

"Nothing."

Nothing?

"Nothing. We just want you to go about the business of fulfilling your potential so we can enjoy you."

Yes!

"And be proud of you."

Yes!

"Because, let's face it—if we don't get ourselves a

kid now, when *will* we do it? When we're old folks? No."

True!

"When we're floe folks? Of course not."

Who?

"So all the money, *and* my harpoon collection, *and* my pelt-cleaning establishment are yours."

"Excuse me, Momma and Poppa Chill, but what are floe folks?"

"North, Eskimo folks are extremely proud folks who dedicate their lives to the Arctic community. So when a proud Eskimo becomes too old or too weak to contribute to our society, well, rather than just sit around and collect frost, he is placed on an ice floe and is proudly set out to sea."

"To die?"

"With honor. Everything we do is with pride and honor. And it will be our honor to have you sign this contract, which will make you our son, as well as a source of pride to Eskimos the world over," said Poppa Chill as he unzipped his down coat, unsnapped his down vest, and pulled up his down sweater before proceeding to unfasten, undo, unbutton, untie, and un-Velcro all twenty-seven of the down, flannel, wool, sports, sweat, and undershirts he was wearing—before producing the contract that was stuffed inside the thermos that was taped to his hairy chest.

"You should feel very honored," Momma Chill said to North.

And he did. He really did. However, there was one small problem: North wanted a no-floe clause in his contract. And hey, who could blame him?

How could any son sleep at night (let alone perform to the best of his ability) knowing that if he broke an ankle while running errands on a glacier or if he fractured his skull by accidentally skating into a polar cap or . . . Oh, it was so easy for North to envision the whole scene.

The Pole Bowl. Yes, it's North vs. everyone from the South Pole. They're playing hockey, Arctic hockey. Everyone is riding penguins, and instead of a puck, it's a reindeer's bladder they're trying to get into the other side's net. North (who, then?) is the goalie, and he watches as the entire team from the South bears down on him. Hundreds and hundreds of opposing players who are understandably weary from this contest that's taken a full Arctic day (six months!) to play, but who somehow conjure up a burst of energy because the stakes they're playing for are quite high, in that the losers have to shovel the winners' driveways for a whole Arctic year (two days!). Ten–9–8–7 . . . Time is running out as the South moves in for the final shot . . . 6–5–4 . . . "Cool Hand" North puts down his iced tea, picks up his hockey stick and . . . 3–2–1 . . . the South shoots and . . . it's stopped by North! Yes, it's a 1–0 victory and the Eskimos are going wild—shaking hands, rubbing noses, winterizing cars—when all of a sudden . . . wait a second . . . what's this? . . . North is down! He's hurt. The "Pride of the Huskies" is lying prone on the ice and, as if on cue, all the spectators leave their seats and make way for the fallen boy. Sure, it's only a minor flesh wound, but these Eskimo folks tend to be overreacting folks, and they demonstrate this by descending onto the rink and hoisting North onto their shoulders, and (despite his cries of "I'm okay! Hey, I'm okay!") they set him adrift without so much as saying "Good game."

No! They couldn't have it both ways. They just couldn't. Look, if North fulfilled his potential—that would be great for him, and great for the Eskimos. However, if he should hurt himself in the process, shouldn't a kid expect his folks to be appreciative nonetheless and help nurse him back to health? Yes! Shouldn't they be proud of him *even* if he could no longer produce the numbers he once did? Yes! Hey, did the Dodgers shoot Campy after that accident? No! Did Ward and June threaten to snuff the life out of Beaver whenever he got a bad report card? No! Did North get that no-floe clause?

"No! It's unheard of," said Poppa Chill.

"Then the deal's off," said North.

"You've got the backbone of a Hawaiian," cried Poppa Chill.

North first noticed it as his plane was making its final descent. The coughing noise, followed by the spewing of smoke. Dense black billows that emanated not from the plane (thank goodness!), but from something on the ground. A continuous flow of dark clouds that wafted skyward, with a relentless momentum that now threatened to engulf the entire plane.

"Nothing to worry about . . . I think," offered the pilot, who had every hope that if he changed course and approached the runway from the other direction, he could safely land behind the belching source of this mess.

Bracing himself in his seat by the window, a white-knuckled North felt completely helpless as the plane banked to the left, then to the right, then to the left, blindly groping its way through this thick dark fog.

North had lived through this scene before, but only as a viewer of those old black-and-white World War II movies where the pilot is blinded but lands the plane safely after someone tells him what to do and not to worry. But now that North was actually living this scene (and in color, no less), he had no choice but to worry because he didn't like either the color *or* the

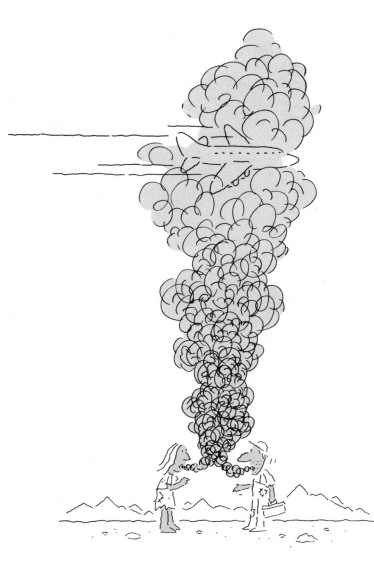

odor of the ashen wall of soot that threatened to . . .
wait a second . . . hold on, one more second . . . yes!
Clear skies! The pilot's plan had worked, and not only
was everyone safe but North was now able to look out
his window and see who was responsible for this near-
tragedy. It was two people. Two smoke-belching people.

"Stewardess, please tell the pilot not to land here."

"Are you sure, North?"

"Yes, I'm sure."

North sat back in his seat, shook his head, and
sighed. But as much as it saddened him, he knew that
he'd made the right decision. Oh well, so much for
the West Virginia folks (the coal-mining folks, the
black-lung folks).

No, North was not starting to get discouraged.
There was no reason to. First of all, he was not even
halfway through his list. And, as was his style, he'd
saved the best folks (the circus folks!) for the very last.

You see, North always saved the best things for the
very last. Take dessert, for example. Dessert was always the highlight of any meal. But wasn't it intelli-
gent culinary strategy to look forward to it during the
entire dinner—as opposed to peaking early and having nothing to look forward to except trying to deal
with whatever sludge was on the plate in front of you?
Of course it was. And North chose to employ this same
tactic when devising the order in which he was going
to visit all these prospective folks. So on both an intel-
lectual and a rational level, it made perfect sense that
things were going to get better. No, there was nothing
to worry about.

Next stop:

"A kid like you can own this town. You really can."

Yes, the urban folks were city folks (Yankee folks, Doodle-Dandy folks), and they really meant it when they said, "If you can make it here, you can make it anywhere."

"This is the media capital of the world," said Doodle Daddy. "You can go to school from September to June, then star in a show and have a candy bar named after you in the summer."

A NOTE TO DENTISTS:

Fear not. North appreciated the importance of dental hygiene and was always a heralded warrior in the fight against tooth decay. Therefore, he would *never* lend his name to any confectionary product that (in addition to chocolate, caramel, peanuts, cashews, raisins, and marshmallows) didn't have fluoride as one of the ingredients.

"Here's your bonus," said Doodle Daddy, as he handed North a roll of bills that could've choked Secretariat.

"But I haven't signed with you yet."

"Doesn't matter," said Doodle Daddy. "You're a winner and that's what *does* matter. Keep it." They were dining at Le Melting Pot—one of the city's most elegant international restaurants.

"This city has eight million people, all of whom have a different story and all of whom are writing screenplays based on those stories. People here are fighting and struggling to become something other than what they are, but only the strongest survive," said Doodle Daddy, before biting into a slice of Pizza Tempura Chevalier.

"I'm a suburban kid myself," said North, trying his best to pick up his hot dog with those chopsticks they gave him. You see, before this visit, North had been to the city only on special occasions with his original folks or on field trips with his class—but he was quite aware of the advantages that a thriving metropolis had to offer.

"Now, we can send you to a private school *or* we can outfit you with a suit of armor so you don't get dismembered by any of the kinds of kids who attend our city's public schools. But we don't have to decide that, or make *any* binding decisions about anything right now. What *is* important is the history of we, the Yankee folks. It's a great, winning tradition that I want you to be a part of."

The Yankee tradition. Yes!

"Please consider joining our family."

And, later that very night, North did just that. He considered. Or at least he made a concerted effort to, before his concentration was broken by the sound of pebbles tapping against his window. Now, ordinarily North would never allow any "Hey, Spanky, it's me, Alfalfa—come on out and let's see what Buckwheat's up to" pebbles-tapping-against-the-window routine to interrupt any heavy consideration that he was into. But under these circumstances, he just had to pay attention. Hey, he was on the forty-seventh floor of a high-rise apartment building—so who could blame him for questioning such an occurrence?

So in an attempt not to get caught sneaking out in the middle of the night, North tied one hundred and fifty bedsheets together and lowered himself down the outside of the skyscraper, where he discovered a young boy, about his age, standing on the sidewalk selling pencils.

"I see they gave you my old room."

"*Your* old room? Who are you?" asked North.

"Doodle Denny."

"Doodle who?"

"Doodle Denny. And I came to warn you."

"About what?"

"My *ex*-father. Don't trust him."

"Your ex-father?"

"He adopted me a few years ago. He couldn't have kids of his own. Something about shrapnel."

"Shrapnel?"

"And everything was going great until—"

"Hey, how do I know you're telling the truth? How do I know that you even *know* Doodle Daddy?"

"You had dinner with him tonight. He took you around town, telling you that you were perfect to carry on the Yankee tradition."

"Yeah, but—"

"Did you pay close attention to him while he was speaking?"

"Yes."

"Okay, now I'm going to take one of these pencils and write down a number on this piece of paper. Then, I want you to tell me which side of his mouth he was talking out of. And if what you say matches what I've written, *then* will you believe me?"

"Of course."

"Okay. I've written down a number. Go ahead."

"Doodle Daddy spoke out of *both* sides of his mouth." And with that, the boy unfolded his piece of paper, upon which was written the number 2. The boy wasn't lying! He *was* Doodle Denny.

"My ex-dad will wine and dine you, but when it really comes down to it, he won't let you have a moment's peace. He second-guesses everything you do. He phones you at school and tells you what to do on multiple-choice tests."

"He does?"

"Yes. And do you realize that he used to sit on the bench with me and my piano teacher?"

"He did?"

"That's right. I also had eight different Doodle Mammies in the five years that I lived with him."

"Divorce?"

"No. He fired them. Some of them outright, and some of them were given other positions in the family. For example, one of my dismissed mothers is now my nephew. It's all so very complicated."

"And what about you?"

"He had my adoption annulled."

"I'm so sorry . . ."

"You just can't win with him. If you do well, he takes the credit. And if you hurt your arm, as I did, you're gone. He's originally from Ohio, but he's very much like an Eskimo when it comes to those kinds of things."

"You hurt your arm? Hey, you just thew a pebble forty-seven floors."

Doodle Denny hung his head and wiped a small tear from the corner of his eye. "Last year I was able to hit the Space Shuttle."

The next flight was a long one. It was transcontinental, so how could it be anything but? Doodle Denny had made his point. If his ex-father placed those kinds of demands on his family, well, good logic dictated that Doodle Daddy would eventually become *North's* ex-father, too.

Who needed it? The discipline. The constant sur-

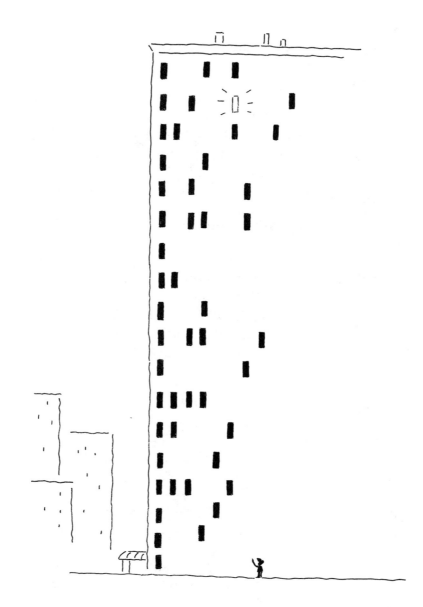

veillance. The kind of regimentation one usually associates with our armed forces. No, Doodle Daddy's life was too strict for North. Far too strict. So, like the proverbial pendulum, North's plane swung from that extreme, 180 degrees across the country, to the rock side of the parental coin.

"Boy Dad?"

Yes, the L.A. folks were new wave folks (rebellious folks, high-decibel folks), and when North went to shake hands, Boy Dad slam-danced him into a car parked on the Sunset Strip.

"I'm sorry, North. But you'll have to excuse me. I've been up for five months straight, so I'm a little spaced."

North peeled himself off the side of someone's Rolls-Royce.

"Five months?"

"Yeah, like we've been shooting my new video and we've had to wait for the seasons to change."

"But aren't all the seasons the same in L.A.?"

"Well, that's the problem!" shouted Boy Dad as he picked North up and threw him against the wall of a producer's mansion.

"Boy Dad?"

"Yeah."

"Is there a place we can go sit and talk? My back is starting to hurt."

"No problem," said Boy Dad as he hit North in the chest with his synthesizer. "Let's go to my apartment."

So North got into Boy Dad's convertible, whose paint job reminded him of poison oak, and they drove along the Sunset Strip.

Oh, how North was hoping that things would work out with these L.A. folks! And why shouldn't they? Shouldn't it be easy for a kid to get along with folks who are only a few years older than the kid himself?

Wasn't it rock songs that North sang as well as anyone? Wasn't it about time that North unveiled those
hard rock moves whose exposure, up until now, had
been limited to the small area in front of his bedroom
mirror? Hey, wasn't it time for Kid North?

Yes, Kid North . . . Kid North . . . Kid North . . .

The convertible continued along the Sunset Strip
until it made a surrealistic turn onto MTV Way—a hi-
tech road where North imagined a dreadlocked Kid
North performing with businessmen who were dancing on a foggy beach, street gangs who were singing
in a zoo, churches that were laughing, astronauts who
were clapping, a candle that was in jail, Beethoven,
and two black-and-white drummers who lived inside a
burning sombrero—before Boy Dad did a handstand
on the brakes and sent Kid North flying, in slow motion, back into reality . . . and through the bay window
of his second-story apartment.

And what an apartment it was! Purple walls, plati-
num records, antique furniture (from the '60s!) and
orange carpeting that was vacuumed in such a way
that there was a mohawk running down the middle of
the kitchen floor.

Boy Dad handed North a keg of beer and then said,
"Look, we've got money, so you've got money. And
we've got no discipline, so you can raise yourself. Do
what you have to do. Here are some chains—go trash
your school."

"I can't do that."

"I like that."

"You like what?"

"That I'm not even your father yet and you're already rebelling."

"I'm not rebelling."

"See? You just did it again."

"But disagreeing isn't rebelling."

"I disagree."

"So do I."

"I like that."

"Boy Dad, you're starting to repeat yourself."

"So, would you like to meet Whammo?"

But before North even had a chance to say yes, he would like to meet his prospective mom, the bald-headed Whammo came roaring into the living room on a motorcycle and screeched to a halt just before extending her hand to North, which he grabbed just before she started up the engine again and dragged him around the room, just before letting go of his hand and sending him flying into a pile of those huge safety pins that punk folks wear in their noses.

North got up. Not in slow motion this time, but slowly nonetheless. Was this what he wanted? Sure, Doodle Daddy may have been too strict, but was *this* what he was looking for in a domestic situation?

"I like that," said Whammo. "He's only known me a few minutes and already he's thinking of leaving us."

"Didn't I tell you he was great?" said Boy Dad as he and Whammo each took one of North's legs, lifted him up and threw him against someone's road manager. "Oh, we're gonna have such a great time together," he continued.

"I disagree," said North.

"Sorry to keep you on hold for so long."

"That's okay."

"Now, what did you say your name was again?"

"North."

"North?"

"Yes. This is the third time I've called."

"N-O-R-T-H . . . North . . . Okay. Now, what can I do for you?"

"I'd like to speak to Arthur Belt."

"Oh, well, Mr. Belt isn't here right now. He's at the site of the new mall."

"You mean Jacobie and Belt is going to open another conveniently located office in another suburban mall? That's great. How many does that make? Fifteen? Sixteen?"

"No, you don't understand. The whole mall will be ours. It's the Jacobie and Belt Law Complex for Legal Matters That Are Simple and Complex."

"Good name."

"Yes, so I don't expect him back for some time. Today's the day that they unveil the new sign, so the ceremony might take a while."

"I see."

"And after that, he's got that banquet to go to."

"Banquet?"

"The one over at the Hilton. For Winchell. For winning the Pulitzer."

"Oh."

"Yes, we're all very happy about it. Now, is there a number where Mr. Belt can reach you?"

"No. I'm calling from a phone booth."

"Well, I'll tell him that you called."

"Thank you."

"Say cheese," said the next set of prospective folks —and, right away, North knew that he was in big trouble. You see, if this request were merely the traditional prelude to a snapshot that was about to be taken, then North would've been more than happy to oblige. But when the words "say cheese" were immediately followed by "say milk" and "say butter," well, North couldn't help bending at the knee and silently asking the Lord to grant him the good sense to say "goodbye."

Yes, the Land O' Lakes folks were dairy folks (Grade "A" folks, processed folks); but what drove North crazy was that they smelled like curdled folks. *Never,* but *never,* had North encountered an aroma like this. These Land O' Lakes folks reeked!

Now, granted, North's sense of smell (*in addition to* those of sight, sound, taste, and touch) was so keen that the chance of his detecting even the most subtle hint of any fragrance that went unnoticed by everyone else was always a possibility. And North was more than willing to make that allowance. But as much as he tried his best to give these folks the benefit of every doubt, he knew that he was only kidding himself. North's olfactory prowess notwithstanding, this odor was no subtle hint. This was an announcement. This was a shout through a bullhorn. This was a sour milk/ancient cheese/moldy sweet cream stench that could actually induce Lincoln to sit up in his grave and tip his hat.

"Dairy is our life," said the Cheese Wiz.

"No kidding?" said North, sticking his head out the car window in an attempt to inhale anything that wouldn't pickle his lungs.

"Are you being sarcastic with us?" asked his wife, the Dairy Queen.

North sarcastic?

"No one told us anything about sarcasm."

"And no one told me you were going to stink like this, Ma and Pa Wiz."

"My goodness, isn't *he* insulting?"

North insulting?

"We didn't go through all this trouble of drafting you just to be insulted."

"And I didn't fly all the way to the Land O' Lakes to turn blue. I want folks who need a son, not a hose-down."

Out of character? Absolutely. Even North was surprised by his candor. But he couldn't help it. He really couldn't.

"Look, North, we're just a couple of old dairy folks. Not florists. But if you have a problem with the way we smell, why don't you just turn around and go back home and let us enjoy our odor in peace?"

Go home? North? Not a prayer. At this point, even if he wanted to (which he didn't), he couldn't. You see, the pressure that was on him was tremendous. He no longer was the captain of only *his* fate. Oh, no. If North decided now to curtail his personal mission, he consequently would negate all the progress that the other kids had made. Go home? North? No. He couldn't. He just couldn't.

But on the way to his next stop, one thing North *could* do was keep asking himself the same questions: Hey, what's going on? How could it be that a few short weeks ago things had looked so bright and optimistic

. . . and now, well, now nothing seemed to be going right? What happened? Why the change? Was there really an explanation for this?

North hoped so. He really did.

"To everything there is a season."

Yes, the Amish folks were gentle folks (Bible folks; Turn, Turn, Turn folks), and they turned out in droves, as well as horses and buggies, to escort North home from the airport. You know, North had never really considered becoming a member of a large family. But the moment he saw Mother and Father Clinton, their forty-seven children, and their eleven

hundred grandchildren, well, North couldn't help not feeling so lonely anymore.

The Amish? Was *this* what North was looking for? The Amish? The people who weren't Quakers but who were just as boring in their *own* right. The Amish? North himself was surprised at just how touched he felt to see this familial throng that had taken precious time away from their various chores around the farm

(Churn, Churn, Churn folks!) to welcome him to Lancaster.

Peaceful folks. Pious folks. Could it be? Could it *possibly* be that North would find a home among these black-cloaked folks? How could this be? It defied all predictions, but . . . but, at this point, North figured he'd give it a try.

And try he did. Upon entering the buggy of honor, he tried to eat all the homemade pies and horns o' plenty that were in there. And when he was introduced to his thirty-four new brothers, he tried to keep a straight face when he learned that all their names were Eleazar. And when Father Clinton gave North a tour of the farm and pointed to "wherest thou is going to spend the night," North tried his best to refrain from going for his prospective father's throat.

"Why do I have to sleep strapped to the blade of a turning windmill?"

"For thou art going to be punished."

"But what art did I do?"

"Thou broketh a commandment."

"Whicheth one?"

"Honor thy mother and thy father."

"But I haven't even knoweth you long enough to hath dishonored you and Mother Clinton."

"It is for all mothers and fathers who have loseth their honor because of you."

Amish Catch-22! That's the only way it could be described. If North hadn't left his folks, he would never have been drafted by the Clintons in the first place. And now they were punishing *him* for it? It didn't make sense. None of it did. North looked to Mother Clinton, hoping *she'd* offer a voice of reason. But she didn't. She couldn't. She was too busy greasing a plow with butter that she was applying with a biscuit.

And that's when it happened. That's when North turn, turn, turned on his heels and started running.

That's right. Running. It was totally spontaneous, without design or premeditated purpose. And it surprised even North himself. But before he knew it, he was in full stride. Running. Away. Not toward anything in particular, but away from everything in general. So fast that he actually ran out from under his baseball cap. But he made no effort even to stop and retrieve it. No. At this point he couldn't stop for anything. It was no longer possible. He was like a racehorse that crosses the finish line but will keep on running until it drops—unless the jockey pulls back on the reins and brings it to a halt. And that's what North was like right now. Fueled by frustration and propelled by desperation, North was picking up a full head of steam and his velocity was increasing accordingly. One small difference between North and those racehorses, though. There was no jockey sitting on North's back to induce him to stop—even if there had been anyone or anything worth stopping for. So North kept running. Mile after mile. Through town after town. And he didn't come to a full stop until he passed a small roadside travel lodge where, from inside, North heard a sound he hadn't heard in quite a while.

Laughter.

CHAPTER

7

His name was Joey Fingers and he made folks laugh. All kinds of folks. Take the folks who were sitting in this nightclub lounge, for instance. Young folks, old folks, out-of-town folks, transient folks . . . all of them (and there were lots of them) just couldn't seem to get enough of this comical little man with grayish stubble on his smiling face. You know the face. At one time that face was probably even smaller than it was today, except that now the flesh on his chin and cheeks had earned the right to relax after all those years of faithful service. And the faces of the folks in the audience? Well, they were nothing but contorted testimonies to the glee that this little man—who was singing and dancing and telling all kinds of jokes and riddles—was providing them with.

After the show, North went backstage to Joey Fingers's dressing room.

"How do you do it?" North asked. "How do you make all these people laugh so hard?"

"It's easy when you have a sense of humor. And I have a sense of humor. And so does my dentist," said Joey Fingers, who then pulled a lot of Chiclets out of his mouth, making believe they were his teeth. "You

can do anything when you have a sense of humor. Hi,
I'm Joey Fingers. And your name is . . ."

North couldn't believe his ears. "You mean you
don't know?" he asked.

"Oh, that's a funny thing to do," said Joey Fingers.
"Making like someone should know you is a very
funny idea."

"But I'm North."

"And that's a very funny name. You're good, kid."

"I'm the kid that you've been reading about in all
the newspapers."

"But you want to hear something that's *really*
funny?" Joey Fingers looked around and then said this
next sentence sort of confidentially. "I can't *remember*
the last time I read a newspaper." Joey Fingers held
up his right hand as if he were taking an oath. "True
story. What's the sense? Nothing's new. It never is."

"But—"

"But let that be our secret, okay? Because if everyone found out that nothing is new, they'd stop laughing."

"Why?"

"Because they'd say they'd heard it before."

North looked into the eyes of Joey Fingers and, for
some reason, he believed him. He believed that Joey
Fingers didn't know who he was and he believed
that Joey Fingers really didn't care. But North liked
this switch. And he felt tremendously honored when
this funny little man who only talked about things that
were funny asked him if he'd like to travel with him
to his next job (Ramada!).

So North now found himself traveling up the turnpike in Joey Fingers's car.

"You see, there has to be a two-way street with your
audience. If you want folks to laugh, you have to say
things that they think are funny."

"But don't you have to get their attention so they'll listen to you in the first place?"

"Of course."

"That's where I have my problem," North confessed.

Joey Fingers looked at North and smiled. "What's your technique?"

"Heart attacks."

"Funny idea."

"My whole body stiffens and then jerks . . ."

"But physical shtick just isn't enough. Especially for openers. It's too much too soon. Look, everyone who does what we do is saying the same thing. They're saying, 'Look at me. Look at me.' But you can't come right out and hit your audience over the head with that. They'll eat you up alive. You gotta make *them* feel comfortable first."

"But I tried everything . . ."

"Here, let me show you."

Slowing down as they approached the toll plaza, Joey Fingers held the steering wheel with his left hand while he leaned back and reached into his pants pocket and pulled out a quarter with his other hand.

"Okay, now you try your physical thing and let's see how it works," said Joey Fingers, handing North the quarter.

"You want me to have a coronary in front of the toll collector?"

"Anything physical. Go ahead. Give it your best shot."

Never one to walk away from a challenge, North accepted the quarter, got out of his side of the car, and, before relinquishing the coin to the outstretched hand of the man in the booth, really went to town. He bowed at the waist; straightened up; shook the toll collector's hand; removed the man's watch and wed-

ding ring; threw those items into the air; smiled; removed the man's eyeglasses and threw *them* into the
air; called the man a "knucklehead"; dropped to the
pavement and started spinning in a bicyclelike motion
on the side of his hip while making a "woo-woo" sound
like Curly of the Three Stooges; stood up; kissed the
toll collector on the lips; caught the eyeglasses, watch,
and wedding ring before they hit the ground; deftly
put them all in their proper places on the toll collector's person; and kissed him once again before actually handing him the coin that guaranteed further
passage along this turnpike.

What a performance! Bravo! An incredible routine,
which one rarely gets to see on *any* of our nation's
great highways. And just how did the toll collector
respond to this? Just how did he display his appreciation for North's attempt to inject a little variety into a
transaction whose dynamics very rarely include slap-
stick? Well, he nodded, smiled, then took out his pistol
and fired six shots into the left front tire of Joey Fingers's car.

"So much for opening with physical shtick. Now,
let's try it my way," said Joey Fingers as he reached
into his pocket and pulled out another quarter. He
then guided his wounded auto through a slow, sweep-
ing U-turn and came to a stop at a toll booth that
accepted fares from those motorists going in the other
direction. Joey Fingers then handed this civil servant
the coin in what can only be described as a most civil
manner.

"Thank you," said the toll collector.

"You're quite welcome," said Joey Fingers.

"Big deal," said North.

"Who said I'm finished?" asked Joey Fingers as he
pulled out still another quarter, steered the car
through still another U-turn, and hobbled to a stop in

the lane of the toll collector whose gun was still smoking. Joey Fingers looked across the seat, winked at North, then turned his attention to his hostile audience.

"That's some gun that you got there. But you know something? On you, it looks good. Me? No, I'd look silly with such a thing. But in your hands, knock wood, it looks good . . . But then again, why shouldn't it look good? *You* look good. Nice hair. Nice hat. Strong chin . . . On you, that blue uniform looks good. On me? What can I say? A blue uniform makes me look like a vein. But you? Where you from?"

"Jersey."

"Jersey? . . . *New* Jersey?"

"New Jersey."

"New Jersey . . . nice place if you're a fart." The toll collector laughed. But that didn't stop Joey Fingers.

"Ah, ah, ah . . . I'll have none of that. No laughing. I'm a comic and laughing ruins my timing, so I don't want to hear any laughing. What's that you're drinking?" The toll collector had a cup of ice cold soda on the shelf in his booth.

"Soda."

"You're sure?"

"Yes, I'm sure."

"You're sure it's not booze?"

"Yes, I'm sure."

"Good boy. Don't drink. It's not good for you."

"Okay."

"I had an uncle who drank. He was a hero. During the war, they put a match to his liver and dropped it over Dresden. So do me a favor. Don't drink."

North couldn't believe it! The toll collector was laughing, the other drivers were honking their horns in appreciation, and North himself was giggling so hard that he had to hold his stomach. That's right.

North was laughing. The same North who hadn't had a good chuckle since Winchell got mono in third grade.

"Thank you. Thank you very much." Joey Fingers bowed, pressed the quarter into the hand of the toll collector (who insisted on changing the tire he had shot), waved to the other motorists, and said "Good night" before getting back into the car and driving away.

"That was great," said North.

"Oh, I could have gone on longer, but it's good to leave them while they're still laughing because that's how they'll remember you—as someone who made them laugh. It's important to know when to quit. But those jokes that I did—"

"Yes?"

"I've been doing some of those jokes since vaudeville."

"Are you kidding, Joey?"

"Nope. I first did those jokes in Chicago. The Jupiter Theater. I was on the same bill with Lockjaw and Phillips. Remember them?"

"Lockjaw and who?"

"How old are you?"

"Nine."

"Oh, well, this was before your time. It was a great act. You see, Lockjaw would bend down and pick up a kitchen table with his teeth—and hold it in midair while his partner, Phillips, would sit on top of it and play the cello." North found himself laughing again. "That's what I'm trying to tell you. If something is funny, it's always funny. Let's say you make a funny joke about a president, right? And then, four years later there's a new president. So what do you do— throw the joke out? No. You take the new president's name, attach it to the same joke, and people still laugh. People don't change. They just think they do. But remember, that's our secret."

So it came to pass that North and Joey Fingers started to travel around together. From inn to inn, from hotel to motel, North watched how Joey Fingers made all conceivable types of folks laugh themselves silly. And after they did, they'd come up to him in the bar or in the coffee shop and thank him for all the laughs and then tell this seventy-six-year-old man that they just knew he was going to be a star some day. And North just knew it, too.

"It's going to happen, Joey."

But Joey Fingers would only smile and say, "If it happens, it happens."

However, North grew to believe that his new friend could make *anything* happen. Except going home, that is.

You see, Joey Fingers was not from here at all. No, he was from the Old Country. North himself wasn't quite sure where this Old Country was, but good logic led him to conclude that, wherever it was, it must be pretty old, considering how old Joey Fingers was. As a matter of fact, "Joey Fingers" wasn't even his real name. It was *Joseph* Fingers! It's just that when he came to this country by himself—in that boat—the man at Ellis Island didn't know how to pronounce "Joseph," so he wrote "Joey" down on the papers and the name just stuck.

This all had taken place when Joey Fingers was approximately North's age, but Joey wasn't really sure of the exact date. He didn't even know when his birth-day was! All he remembered was that a long time ago, on his last birthday in the Old Country, there was a great big party. And his Mom and Dad and brothers and sisters and all the townsfolk were there; and it was fun and there was dancing and then right in the middle of everything, the men on the horses came and . . . and . . .

"All I remember is that it was snowing. So whenever it snows, I think it's my birthday. It's an easy way to keep track. Last winter I had fourteen birthdays."

"Is your wife also from the Old Country?"

"What wife? Who has a wife?"

"The wife you always make jokes about . . . The one who has a headache every night? The one who's so fat that she has her own zip code."

"I never had a wife."

"But . . ."

"Those are only jokes."

"So how did you get all those children? Your son who married the tramp? Your granddaughter who has all those pimples?"

"All of those are jokes. Good jokes. But jokes."

"And your original family?"

"That I don't joke about. That's not funny."

"I'm sorry . . ."

"But it will be once I get home."

"To the Old Country?"

"Then we'll joke again. Then we'll continue with our lives."

Such was the story of Joey Fingers. Oh, thought North, if only Joey Fingers knew, back then in the Old Country, what he now knows about playing to difficult audiences. Perhaps he could have handled the whole situation with those hostile folks who plundered and pillaged and hurt the people whom Joey loved most.

But what saddened North even more was the thought of this little man, who went all over making everyone so happy, actually putting his own life on hold for over seven decades. This just didn't seem fair. It really didn't.

"Records are made to be broken. They truly are. But if *this* record is ever broken, I'll be very surprised."

Yes, the speaker was Guinness. And yes, North's folks were just about to gain entry into his *Book of World Records*.

Midafternoon. A small crowd was milling around a particular display case at the Smithsonian. Fifty-seven days ago North's folks had been transported from Judge Buckle's chambers and they had been lying dormant in the Hall of Minerals ever since. Dressed formally for this occasion by the curator himself, they now stood propped up on hand trucks, oblivious to the digital clock ticking off the weeks, days, seconds, and then . . .

"Ladies and gentlemen, North's Mom and Dad have just broken the all-time record for 'consecutive days spent sleeping in a national museum.' "

There was a smattering of applause from those who came to witness Mom and Dad's special day. But one man not only didn't applaud but refused to have his picture taken alongside the new champs.

"It's not fair," said a pouting Joe D. "It's just not fair."

"Come on, Joe," exhorted Guinness. "Don't be such a sore sport. North's folks beat your record fair and square."

"Fair and square? In 1941 I got at least one hit in fifty-six consecutive major league baseball games."

"Right . . ."

"And all these people have been doing is sleep-ing—"

"For *fifty-seven* consecutive days."

"But shouldn't that be in a *different* category?

NORTH'S FOLKS

Sleeping in a museum and playing baseball are two completely different things."

"Joe, I hate to say this, but I think you're being petty."

Guinness grabbed Joltin' Joe's arm and took him aside so they could talk confidentially.

"Joe, we're old friends. What's really bothering you?"

"I'm sorry, Guinness. I don't want to sound bitter—"

"But . . ."

"It's just that sixty years ago, I was twice the ballplayer *and* a better son than any of these kids today."

"I'm sure you were."

"Oh, I'm not complaining, Guinness. But if North really got the kinds of offers that I've been reading about, can you imagine what *I'd* be worth in today's market?"

Guinness could only nod his head and put his arm around a weeping Joe D.

"It's a new world, Joe. It's a new world."

It *was* a new world. And North was trying his best to conquer it.

"Hey, I just got back from Las Vegas, and, boy, are my arms tired."

"Why?"

"What do you mean, Joey?"

"I mean, why are your arms tired?"

"Because I just got back from Las Vegas."

"So?"

"What do you mean, 'So'?"

"North, are your arms tired because of the slot machines or because you carried your own luggage or because you were arm wrestling on the plane, or—"

"No!"

"No, what?"

"I didn't take a plane."

"You didn't?"

"No—that's the joke. I flew in from Las Vegas. *I flew in.*"

"Oh, so *you* flew in."

"Yes."

"Well, why didn't you say so in the first place? At the beginning of the joke?"

"Oh, I get it."

"I don't get it," said the Hojo Hotel entertainment director. "I just don't get it."

North was doing his best not to lose his patience. And who could blame him? Why would anyone *want* to lose his patience because of a hotel entertainment director?

"But I told you three times. All I want you to do is—"

"I heard what you said, son. You want me to give this money to Fingers, right?"

"Right."

"Give it to him after he does his act, right?"

"Yes. And then I want you to read that speech I wrote, but make believe I had nothing to do with it."

"Right. But I still don't get it."

With all due respect, you really couldn't fault the entertainment director for not fully comprehending what North had in mind. You see, traditionally those who entertain at the Hojo Lounge were paid by check, not cash. Furthermore, those entertainers tradition-ally were not paid this much money—enough to choke Secretariat—for their one-night efforts (even if they performed in the main room). But North had always been the type to drive a hard bargain, so when he reached into his pocket and slipped the entertain-ment director a few crumpled remnants of what orig-inally had been the bonus from Doodle Daddy, it miraculously made things clearer.

"I still don't get it, but I'll do it."

As usual, Joey Fingers was simply hysterical that evening at the Hojo Hotel, whose marquee welcomed Elks, Moose, Kiwanis, Rotarians, Shriners, and just about every group of silly-looking, fez-wearing folks. Joey sang, danced, told great jokes, and, when the house lights came up after his closing story about those three Arabs who fell off the rabbi the day before the holiday when Jewish people were not permitted to sneeze, Joey Fingers was more surprised than anyone when the entertainment director strode onstage, ap-proached the microphone, and beckoned Joey Fingers to come back out for still another bow.

"What's he doing?" Joey Fingers asked North in the wings.

"He wants you to go back out there."

"Bad idea. I left them laughing."

"So?"

"So? I told you that it's important to know when to quit."

"Well, maybe it's something important."

"What could be more important than doing a nice, tight show that makes people happy?"

"Joey . . ."

"North, I can't top myself."

"Please . . ."

Suppressing every instinct and compromising every better judgment, Joey Fingers returned to the center of the stage and acknowledged the diminishing applause of those who weren't quite sure why they were being asked to retake their seats even though the show was over.

"Ladies and gentlemen," the entertainment director said into the microphone. "I have a special announcement to make." And with that the entertainment director just stood there, smiling (for what everyone unanimously agreed felt like an eternity), before it dawned on him that he really should make the announcement he had just threatened to make.

"Ladies and gentlemen. Yes, this is very unusual. And yes, it's not a very good idea to call a comic back onstage because he could wear out his welcome. But that couldn't ever happen here because, Joey, you are always welcome. But before anyone says 'You're welcome,' someone usually says 'Thank you.' And that's what we'd like to do now. Everyone here and at all the other Hojo hotels, motels, travel lodges, inns, coffee shops, and rest stops would like to say 'Thank you, Joey Fingers' for all these years that you've been making us laugh. And, as a token of our gratitude, we've taken up a little collection among the busboys and waiters and bellboys, who each kicked in a little something to show their appreciation. Now, wasn't that nice?"

Some scattered applause ran through the room. The entertainment director wasn't finished reading, however.

"But, Joey, they insist you accept this on one condition. That you take this money and treat yourself to a trip back to the Old Country so you can continue with your life."

Yes! And it really didn't matter that no one in the audience, *as well as* the entertainment director, even had a clue as to what that last part of the announcement meant. What *was* important was that Joey Fingers was finally going home.

"You knew about this all along, didn't you?"

"Well, the waiters and the busboys told me that . . ."

"Thanks, North."

"Hey, Joey . . ."

"Yeah?"

"You sleeping?"

"Not yet."

"Good. Because I have another one. Okay, now . . ." North cleared his throat. "The Old Country is very old."

"How old *is* it?"

"The Old Country is so old that you have to dust the dirt floors with a live chicken."

"Hmmm. . . ."

"What do you think?"

"They're getting better."

"You really think so, Joey?"

"Sure. Now, I have one for you."

"Oh, good."

"What two people should go to sleep because they've got a big day tomorrow?"

"Okay, I get it."

North and Joey Fingers left for the Old Country the very next day. Election Day. Now, traditionally Election Day is the first Tuesday after the first Monday in November. This inalienable right has been an autumn ritual, as set forth by our Founding Fathers, for over 200 years.

Not this year, though. No, this year a November election would have been too late when one considered how much work there was to do. No, when one considered the tedium of setting up voting booths, the tabulation of results, and the orderly transition of an outgoing to an incoming administration, elections had to be held right then if the reins of power were to be officially passed in time for the proposed month-long Halloweenfest in October.

And when one considered that the voting age had already been lowered to eight, and that the average baby-boom family had an average of 2.9 kids, and that there were plenty of "folks without partners"—well, one didn't have to be a political scientist to figure out which side was going to win this election.

Yes, if you were a kid, you had good reason to rejoice—all things considered.

CHAPTER

8

The moment the plane touched ground, North became confused. "Is it possible we've landed in the wrong Old Country, Joey . . . Joey?"
"Joseph."
It made no sense. It really didn't. Except that, standing against a backdrop of glass-paneled sky-scrapers and contorted chrome statues that adorned the plazas of the crowded shopping malls, little Joseph Fingers suddenly seemed even smaller.

"You see, I told you that nothing is ever new. Come, let me show you."

Hey, who was North to argue? This was Joey's birthplace, and as long as his pal wanted to refer to what was undeniably the stock exchange as the "pro-duce stand," and to what was unquestionably a mul-tiplex cinema as "where we bathe our rams," North was willing to play along. And he also went along with his friend when he said "hi" to everyone in the streets and called them by names that North was willing to bet weren't really their names.

What difference did it make? Really. So what if peo-ple looked at him in an odd way when he sang a song in front of the library? Or if motorists honked their car

horns when he danced across the boulevard? Did it really matter? North didn't think so. Joey Fingers was finally home and he was just starting to feel *at* home. And that's what was important.

"And this? This, North, is my house. Come in. Please. Come into my house."

North wiped his feet before entering. Joey took him on a tour.

"My mother's kitchen. My father's table. And this, this is where we sleep. My bed. My sister Anna's. And our younger brother, Daniel—the baby of the family . . ."

The owner of this establishment wasn't quite sure what to do. Here he is, enjoying his lunch, when all of a sudden he looks up and sees a little man giving a young boy a tour of his car wash. They do seem harmless enough; yet . . .

"Hey, old man, get off that lift. You're gonna hurt yourself."

". . . and this is where my Uncle Meyer keeps his milk wagon—"

"Hey, old man—"

"Excuse me, sir, but do I know you?" asked Joey Fingers.

"What?"

"Are you here to see my father?"

"Hey, now look—"

"Because if you are, he isn't home right now. But he will be soon—so you can just wait over there. Thank you, sir."

Joey Fingers paid no attention to the shouts of the owner, though it really didn't matter, as the tour now continued outside the car wash on the driveway entrance.

"Would you like to play Hop, Step, and Czar?"

"How do you play that, Joseph?"

"And you call yourself a little boy," said Joey Fingers with a smile. "Watch."

That's exactly what North did. He watched as Joey Fingers reached into his pocket and pulled out a coin.

"See this kopek?"

Kopek? With George Washington on it?

"Yes, I see the kopek."

"Good."

Joey Fingers took the coin and placed it on a certain spot on the ground.

"Now, if I should either hop *or* step on that kopek, that would be a terrific thing."

"Why?"

"Why? Because it will mean that I've landed on the Czar's back—snapping his spinal cord, thus rendering him powerless to invade this village. That's why."

"Oh."

"I'll show you."

So North took a seat on the bench and watched as Joey Fingers stood about four paces away from the coin, stared at it, took a deep breath, closed his eyes, mumbled something to himself, opened his eyes, and—with a spryness that is usually specific to little boys—he sprung into the air with a hop, step, and . . .

"You did it! You broke the Czar's back!"

"So I did. So I did." Joey Fingers smiled as he took a seat next to North.

"Do it again, Joseph. Let's see you do it again," begged North, who was so happy, he was laughing. But Joey Fingers shook his head.

"I keep telling you, the most important thing for a comic is to know when to get off."

"Okay. But *now* what do you want to do?"

"Now . . . now it's time for me to continue with my life."

Those were Joey Fingers's last words.

For reasons that were inexplicable to everyone, the moment Joey Fingers closed his eyes forever, it started to snow inside the car wash. Yes, there is lots of water that rains down in a car wash. And yes, when rain is exposed to a sudden drop in temperature (which is not unusual, considering the Ol' Countra winds that blow through the Old Country at this particular time of year), it *can* turn to snow. However, North chose not to delve into the literal explanation for such a phenomenon. There was no need to. So all he did was look at the smiling form of the little man who had made him laugh, and who was now making him cry, and say, "Happy Birthday, Joseph Fingers."

North had never made funeral arrangements before, but the man who owned the car wash was more than helpful. Sure, at first there was a great deal of resistance on his part to having a small-time comic buried in the driveway to his car-washing establishment.

"What are you, nuts? Not for a million bucks." And with that, North took out what was left of his Doodle

Daddy bonus money and stuck it into the till whose sign read TIPS FOR THE BOYS.

"Please, mister . . . Joey Fingers was my friend."

Suffice it to say that as modern as the Old Country was, no one had ever witnessed a Glo-coat burial like this before. Small, simple, tasteful, and on the exact spot that Joey Fingers had wanted to continue his life from. North was certain that Joey would've wanted it this way.

And what about North? Well, for the first time in quite a while, he felt lonely. Not the kind of loneliness that instigates a search for companionship as much as that feeling of emptiness when there's been a loss, the loss of a friend and the spirit he takes with him when he dies. Joey Fingers was now at peace—in union with that part of his soul that would make him complete. As for North, well, he too was looking for something, *anything*: a sign, *any sign*, that would give him hope, purpose, and even direction.

It came from the gravedigger. The sign, that is. It came from the gravedigger, who was perspiring. You see, when the worker who'd just covered Joey Fingers's final resting place with the last spadeful of soil started perspiring as if there were no tomorrow, he proceeded to do what any sensible, sweating gravedigger does at a time like this—he leaned against his shovel, removed a glove from his right hand, inserted that same right hand into his right back pocket, pulled out a crumpled handkerchief, and wiped his brow.

Now, perhaps this seems like a very mundane occurrence that doesn't warrant the waste of both time and book space to recount so vividly its every detail. However, this action did not go unnoticed by North; nor did the slip of paper that accidentally fell from the worker's pocket when he removed his hanky. Not five

minutes had passed since his best friend had been
interred, and already there was litter on the gravesite.
And it saddened North to think (despite the car-wash
owner's promise to tend to its upkeep) that Joey Fingers's grave would not be kept at its manicured best.

So North bent down and picked up the scrap. "Hey,
mister," he yelled to the gravedigger, "you dropped . . .
oh, my goodness . . ."

"Hey, mister, where'd you get those pants?"
"You like them?"
North's gut reaction to what was unequivocally his
father's scrawl resulted from a complex set of emotions that he chose not to analyze at that moment.
There'd be a time for that later. Now was no time for
such introspection. All he knew was that a sixth sense
was telling him that something was wrong and that
he had to get to the bottom of this and find out where
this gravedigger bought his pants.

"Follow me. I'll show you."

Two Guys From the Old Country Country Store was
one of those general stores that sell everything. Food,
toys, power tools—you name it, and the Two Guys had
it. When North raced inside, it was in the clothing
department that all the commotion was taking place.
It was mobbed—ridiculously packed—with Old
Country clothes buyers whose recently purchased
pants contained #6 inspection tags that said "Help!"

"What's this mean?" and "How can we help?" they

all wanted to know. And who could blame them? To discover such a desperate appeal in the depths of one's trousers can be a very upsetting experience for anyone from *any* country. But even the Two Guys themselves were at a loss for a logical explanation.

"*I* don't know what this means," said the First Guy.

"If the pants fit, why get involved?" offered the Other Guy.

It seemed that these inspection tags were cropping up not only in the Old Country but in all countries where inspected garments were sold—so the Two Guys kept telling everyone that they shouldn't feel singled out.

But while these poor excuses for explanations somehow seemed to mollify this horde of curious pants owners, North was far from satisfied. He just had to get to the bottom of this.

And he did. Yes, the store's newspaper stand provided all the answers.

Chaos! According to all the wire service reports, *North's* old country was quite a sight. Folks in chains! Yes, the kids had taken over and the new administration was acting solely in their behalf. Everyone was encouraged to act silly, traffic cops wore pajamas, the Mayo Clinic had a Ferris wheel, yellow was no longer a primary color, and plans were already under way to change the names of state capitals to those of game-show hosts, i.e., "Providence, Rhode Island" was going to become "Bill, Cullen." Yes! Everything was great!

But now everyone back home was really upset. North (the Great Emancipator) had not been heard from in weeks and all the kids (the Great Emancipa-tees) feared for their liberator's well-being. Had he been abducted? Was he slain? Was it the work of one person? Was there a grassy knoll? These questions were on the lips of all the kids, not only because they were reverentially grateful to North for their present state of power but also because they were worried about the weakening of their position should the har-binger of their freedom indeed be dead.

And the folks? Well, they couldn't have cared less whether North was dead or alive. But they *were* fed up with being enslaved by their offspring. Enough was enough. How much longer could they possibly go on being held at emotional gunpoint, being forced to stoop to depths traditionally reserved for lower forms of life, without feeling *some* loss of dignity? Hey, no folk wants to go down in history as being part of a generation that brought about the *de*generation of self-respect as we know it.

And the kids knew that. The kids knew everything. They heard the rumblings. They knew about the se-cret meetings. They knew that the downtrodden-folks class would most assuredly stage some kind of upris-ing if they were not, at the very least, appeased. Paci-fied. Thrown a bone. That's it—thrown a bone. And just what bone did the ruling elite decide would be the best to throw to these malcontented folks? Easy.

North's folks.

It made perfect sense. Weren't they the reason for this present state of affairs? Wasn't it they that all the other folks cursed every time they found themselves liquidating yet another bond to pay for yet another birthday present or demolishing still another land-mark in favor of yet another dirt bike track? Sure it was. So why not give the masses what they wanted? Let them direct their venom toward those whom they felt were most responsible for their lot. The folks would get a chance to vent their hostility. The kids would keep the upper hand. And all would be fine.

As for North's folks . . . Well, sometimes in order to keep the peace, there has to be an offering.

CHAPTER

9

Here was North's problem. If he were already home, he wouldn't have needed any money to *get* home because he'd be there already. But such was not the case; hence, the problem. Not only was he broke, but the anonymity that he'd originally enjoyed in the Old Country became a major stumbling block when it came to the extension of credit.

"Where are you going?"

"On the plane . . . To take me home."

"Where's your ticket?"

"I'm North. My face is my ticket."

But even when North showed the ticket agent a copy of Winchell's *International Newspaper*, it didn't help. If anything, it made matters worse.

"See? I'm North. I'm famous."

"It says there that you're dead."

"But I'm not."

"So what's everybody afraid of?"

"That I *am* dead."

"That's what scares *me*. And I'm not one who's easily frightened. So if you are dead, can you imagine how it's going to affect the *other* passengers?"

"But I'm not dead."

"Sorry, son, but I can't take that chance."

Why was he doing this? Why was North so determined to get back to the place and to the folks he had run away from to begin with? Well, North was feeling the way any kid feels when he's spent his summer going halfway around the globe in an unsuccessful attempt to find new parents. Tired. Yes, North was emotionally weary from his adventures. And while it was conceivable that he could resume his quest by seeking out the English folks (proper folks, tea-at-four folks), Italian folks (pizza folks, Cinzano folks), or even the South African folks (apartheid folks, U.S. Blacks-ban-the-Olympics-because-of-them folks), what sense did it make? Wouldn't it all be the same? Hadn't he learned that folks, *any* kind of folks, were nothing more than older versions of the same misguided people they were when they were kids? Why shouldn't they be? It's just as Joey Fingers had taught him: "Nothing is new. It might be more. It might be less. It might even be disguised. But it doesn't change."

So North had no fantastic expectations about returning home and finding that his folks had been miraculously transformed into ideal folks (model folks, award-winning folks). Not at all. The best that North *could* hope for, however, was that they, too, had learned something from this experience and that they would, at the very least, be tolerable folks (less self-indulgent folks, nonrepulsive folks).

North knew he was taking a chance. After all, there was no guarantee that they had come to similar conclusions. Hey, there wasn't even a guarantee that his folks would still be living folks (breathing folks, existing folks) unless he hurried home to save them.

Hence, the jumping of turnstiles, the stowing away in the backs of buses, the bolting from taxis whose

meters were still running . . . anything he needed to
do (with total disregard for personal injury or misde-
meanor charges) in order to get to the Old Country's
Federal Express office because he absolutely, posi-
tively had to get back home by 10:30 the next morning. Because, according to Winchell's paper, Mom and
Dad were scheduled to be sacrificed at 11:00.

CHAPTER

10

NORTH'S FOLKS TO TWIST IN WIND

ALTERNATE SIDE OF THE STREET
PARKING SUSPENDED

WBS

alk about a hot ticket! This thing had been sold
out for weeks; it was standing room only (with
the obvious exception of those who were fortunate enough to have seats). Yes, the bloodthirsty
throng of vengeful folks wouldn't have missed this for
anything. And the upper class of kids, who were
mourning the reported death of their fallen leader,
was also on hand at North Memorial Stadium to witness the event.

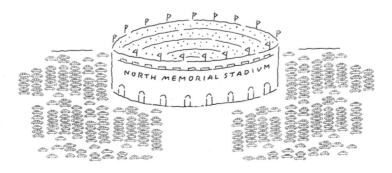

NORTH MEMORIAL STADIUM

They were going to hang Mom and Dad!

That's right, that's all there was to it. It was going to happen. The die was cast. A *fait accompli*. Only a phone call from Governor Belt could save them at this point—but *that* was quite unlikely. You see, legally the decision had already been appealed all the way to the Supreme Court, where it was upheld by Chief Justice Buckle. And commercially, well, all the commercial time had already been sold by the WBS (Winchell Broadcasting System), which had the exclusive television rights to this spectacle. So the stage was set. In thirty minutes North's folks were to hang by their necks—until pronounced dead by Surgeon General Large—and then there'd be peace in the land.

Meanwhile:

What a trip! And, in its own way, an invaluable experience in terms of North's humility. Hey, let's face it—after traveling all over this country *and* to the Old Country first class, what could be more humbling to a kid than being shipped home cargo?

Finally extricating himself from the box he'd been delivered in, a strange feeling overcame North. Yes, it did feel good to be home, but there was something different about the place that he couldn't quite put his finger on at first. Hmm . . . was there new wallpaper? No. Different upholstery? No. The seals, cows, horses, buggies, pineapple trees, grain elevators, goats, coal bins, Picassos, old Eskimos, a lion tamer, etc.—all of which were sent in good faith by the various sets of prospective folks to North's folks as compensation for their boy? Yes! And while it wasn't like North to be rude to guests in his home, under *these* particular circumstances, he really couldn't provide the social amenities he ordinarily would have (chitchat, finger sandwiches, etc.) had things been less hectic. Time was running out. And just what time *was* it?

"Hard to say," said the lion tamer. "You see, the goats ate your folks' clock."

But they hadn't eaten the television. And when North turned it on, he found out exactly what time it was.

"Kill North's folks! Kill North's folks!"

This was the greeting that North's folks received as they emerged from the dugout and were escorted by a cordon of safety patrolmen toward the gallows at the edge of the infield grass. Their hands tied behind them, Mom and Dad seemed groggy. They were yawning. Even the resounding jeers from this torchbearing mob could not totally awaken them from their summer of sedation.

"What's going on?" asked Mom.

"There must be a game today," said Dad.

"Oh."

After the band played the national anthem ("Me and Julio Down by the Schoolyard"), Governor Arthur Belt, looking lean and tan, was smiling and shaking just about everybody's hand as he made his way from his box seat to the WBS microphone that was set up on the platform between Mom and Dad.

"Is this on?" he asked, tapping the mike.

"YES!" answered the throng, in unison.

Governor Belt looked down the first-base line to where all the folks were sitting.

"Ladies and gentlemen, this is a great, great day. See? We're fair. North's Mom and Dad were obnoxious. They caused everyone pain. So they'll be punished."

Cheers, tumultuous cheers, from the crowd.

"Kill 'em . . . Kill 'em . . . Let 'em dangle."

Governor Belt raised his hands over his head in an attempt to silence the enraged mass of folks. He then looked down the third-base line and tried to tell all the kids why he would make an excellent senator. No luck. The chorus of boos and yelps and catcalls that came from the folks drowned him out completely. Oh well. These folks had come here for one reason, and one reason only. So Governor Belt tucked his speech back into his jacket pocket, turned to the executioner (Jacobie!), and said, "Okay, go for it!"

"Wait a second! Hey, wait just one second!" Yes, it was North. And yes, he had just entered the stadium in an Amish buggy—whipping the swayback horse as if it were pulling Ben Hur's chariot.

"Don't kill them! Please don't kill them!" he yelled as he jumped up from the buggy onto the platform where his folks stood, bound and yawning.

"Don't do it!" he yelled again. And then North stopped yelling when he realized that no one recognized him. No one. He'd been away for an entire summer, and hey, he'd grown!

"Who are you?" asked everyone in the stadium.

"It's me . . . North!"

But no one believed him. Kids and folks alike.

"You're not North!"

"North is shorter than you!"

"North is dead!"

"North is dead *and* shorter than you!"

"You're not North!" they all shouted from the stands before the folks resumed their chants of "Kill North's folks! Kill North's folks!" and the kids went back to grieving for their perished savior.

North began to slouch three inches, hoping that everyone would recognize him at his pre–Independence Day height, when his old pal sidled up to him.

"North, my boy."

"Hello, Winchell. How are you?"

"What could be bad? Business is great, I've got a cabin cruiser, a condo in Miami, and I'm not even nine yet."

Winchell was wearing a red carnation in his lapel. North always hated it when Winchell wore red carnations in his lapel. But today North hated it even more. And the way Winchell kept on repeating the phrase "What a day, what a day!" made North come *this* close to vomiting on the gallows. But he didn't. He couldn't. He had a job to do and now was no time to lose his lunch.

The slouching process now complete, North turned back to the throng and screamed into the microphone, "Now do you recognize me? Hey, I'm North!"

The kids' reaction?

"It *is* North."

"He's alive."

"Nor-te! Nor-te! Nor-te!"

The folks' reaction?

"Hey, it *is* North."

"The kid who started this whole thing?"

"The kid who took our pride?"

"The kid who messed up our lives?"

"Yeah, that's the one!"

"Kill North, too! Kill North, too!"

Mom and Dad's reaction?

"Hello, son."

"Hi, Mom."

"How was your summer, son?"

"Not bad. And yours?"

"Restful."

"North?"

"Yes, Dad."

"How come you're not having a coronary?"

"I've learned a few things about relationships this summer, Dad. How about you? Did you and Mom learn anything?"

"It's hard to spend most of the summer in the Smithsonian and *not* learn a thing or two."

North hung his head while saying, "You never took *me* to the Smithsonian."

Dad hung his head while saying, "We did a lot of things wrong, son."

Winchell spoke next. "It won't work, North."

Winchell pointed his finger toward the first-base line.

"Those folks want blood."

He then pointed to the third-base line.

"And the kids have too much to lose. So if you're even thinking of trying to save your parents, forget it."

North looked out at the crowd. Winchell was right.

The folks were chanting "Kill North, too!" even louder than before, and the kids were far too busy celebrating North's return from the dead to even notice that the folks were now leaving their seats and slowly making their way onto the field.

North heard sobbing on the gallows.

"What's wrong, Mom?"

"I'm sorry. It's just that when you were born nine years ago, we were so happy . . . I never dreamed that things would end up like this . . . Your father and I being hanged on national television . . . We really loved you."

"And I loved you, too, Mom."

North was starting to get emotional and Winchell saw this.

"Oh, can't you see that they're just trying to save their necks?"

"Easy, Winchell. This may be taking place in front of hundreds of millions of people, but this is still a private family matter."

As the throng started inching their way toward the gallows, North cried to Mom and Dad.

"Mom, Dad . . ."

"Yes, son . . ."

"I was so mad at you that I never wanted to see you again. And now—"

"And now you'll get your wish," interrupted Winchell. "Don't be stupid, North. Come with us. Live like a king."

"Winchell's right. Hello, North." It was Arthur Belt. "Sorry that I never returned your phone calls, but it's been madness."

"I understand, *Governor*."

"Easy with the attitude, North. You wouldn't want to hang like a *piñata* alongside your folks, would you?"

"You wouldn't dare."

"Oh, wouldn't I?"

"You really think that those kids would allow that to happen to *El Norte*?"

"*El Norte*, huh? Look at those kids, North. Dancing, singing, rejoicing—happy to be alive."

"You mean, happy that *I'm* alive, don't you?"

"Happy that they have whatever freedom they *think* they have. But I can't imagine how *un*happy they'll be if they see that their idol had a change of heart and sided with his folks and tried to take that freedom from them, *El Norte*."

"What do you mean freedom they *think* they have?"

"North?"

"Yes, Winchell?"

"You have a great deal to learn about the spoils of revolution."

"So let me get this straight." It was Judge Buckle who was talking now. Yes, he was confused. And yes, he wanted to get things straight. "If North tries to save his folks, the kids will think he's a traitor and will probably want to hang him for treason. Right?"

"Right," said Arthur Belt.

"And if he tries to save his folks and the kids *don't* hang him, he'll most definitely be ripped to shreds by this advancing horde of vengeful folks who are yelling 'Kill North, too!' Right?"

"Right."

Inching . . . inching . . .

"But if he doesn't try to save his folks and accepts your offer, not only will he be spared but North'll also live in the lap of luxury for the rest of his life. Have I got it right?"

"Yes, you do," answered Arthur Belt.

The chief justice of the Supreme Court looked at North, shrugged his shoulders, and said, "I wish all the decisions I had to make were as cut and dried as this one."

It hit North like a ton of bricks. *His folks were going to die.* What difference did it make whose hands were going to administer the ultimate blow? The end result was going to be identical. Death. The last round-up. The final curtain. And as he looked back at his mom and dad, he was stunned by the prospect that there'd be no opportunity to sit down and calmly talk things over, make the appropriate apologies, heal old wounds, and try to start anew. He really would've liked to. But now he couldn't.

So as the multitude of angry folks inched their way toward the gallows, North just stood there, frozen; he was overwhelmed by the emotions he and his folks were permitting themselves to feel toward each other. The kind of emotions kids and folks rarely convey when they have time to squander. Time to be distracted. And time to be petty. But now it was a different story. Now there was no more time for analysis, misinterpretation, or for speaking through intermediaries. No, now there was only time to lower all guards and let the heart sum things up.

"North."

"Yes, Mom."

"We never meant to hurt you."

"I know."

"We're sorry."

"So am I, Mom."

And, though it wasn't his nature to beg, a very sad North turned to Winchell and said, "Winchell, can you get them off the hook? For old time's sake?"

"*Them* off the hook?"

"Yes!"

"So you're accepting our offer?"

"Winchell, please . . ."

Winchell looked into the eyes of his old prodigal pal. In one eye, he saw his best friend making a simple plea for mercy. In the other eye, he saw a committee of judges melting down his Pulitzer, pouring it into a Nobel Peace Prize mold, letting it cool off, and then presenting it to North.

"Sorry, North, I can't do it."

This time North looked back into the eyes of his sleazy friend, Winchell. In one eye he saw him stealing the Nobel Peace Prize that North had just been awarded in his own eye. In Winchell's other eye North saw his true friend, Joey Fingers, saying that you can do anything when you have a sense of humor.

"I'm glad, Winchell."

"What?"

"I said I'm glad that you're not going to be lenient with my parents."

"You *are* accepting our offer?"

"Look, Winchell, if I'm really honest with myself, I know that my parents don't deserve to live. They really don't. Sure, I rushed back here to save them but . . . just look at this mob. They have every right to be angry. I feel bad how my disagreement with my folks ended up affecting the lives of everyone in this mob. And it's a shame. Because what a fine, fine-looking mob they are. How many of them do you think are from out of town?"

"What kind of question is that?"

North took the microphone off the stand and addressed the throng directly.

"What a mob. What a mob. You're beautiful. Just beautiful. Come on, is anyone here from Jersey? I love New Jersey. I really do. Some of my favorite vigilantes come from there."

The mob's reaction?

"Kill North, too! Kill North, too!"

The kids' reaction? None. They were still singing and dancing among themselves.

Winchell's reaction?

"He's crazy!"

Governor Belt's reaction?

"Let him rant. It's *his* funeral."

North forged ahead.

"Fine mob. Fine mob. Hey, does anyone here have a cigarette? I had a pack but I left it in the machine. Does anyone have a cigarette?"

The mob's reaction? Six flaming torches came flying onto the gallows.

North's reaction? He bent down, picked up one of the torches, walked back to the microphone, and went back to work on his audience.

"Okay. I've got a light, but I still need a cigarette."

The mob's reaction?

"Kill North, too! Kill North, too!"

North's retort?

"You're right. Cigarettes *can* kill you. Can't they, Surgeon General Large? Surgeon General Large, ladies and gentlemen—a surgeon general who is so large that when he sits around the house, he *really* sits around Winchell's yacht."

Winchell's reaction?

"Hey!"

The mob's reaction?

"Kill North, too!"

The kids' reaction?

"Winchell has a *yacht*?"

Yes! North had gotten through to the kids. They stopped dancing. They stopped singing. And they looked toward the gallows for an explanation.

And since he so desperately needed their help to stop the throng of folks who were now at the foot of the gallows, North started to play the kids' side of the stadium.

"Hey, it's nice to hear you respond. For a minute there, I thought you guys had left the place. You know, like you'd hopped aboard Governor Belt's private jet and flown down to Winchell's condominium in Miami . . ."

"Winchell has a condo?"

"Does Winchell have a condo?" North asked rhetorically. "Is the Pope Catholic? Do bears make in the woods? Does Winchell have a butler? Of course Winchell has a condo. In Miami. Lots of old folks live in his condo. It's called the Wrinkled Arms. It's very nice. In the back they have a kidney-shaped swimming pool. And every morning, just to be realistic, they drop a little stone in it. But seriously. Old folks. Young folks! What's the difference?"

"Winchell has a butler?"

North looked at Winchell, whose face was almost as red as the carnation in his lapel. Yes, Winchell was concerned—and he had good reason to be. The kids had now left their seats along the first-base line and were starting to race toward the gallows.

"Hey, I kid Winchell, but I love him. I really do. It's hard not to love a guy who spends countless hours with Governor Belt talking about how all the parents are going to get all their rights and all their dignity back."

The folks' reaction?

"They do?"

The kids' reaction?

"They what?"

Governor Belt's reaction?

"We what?"

Winchell's reaction after looking out at the sea of folks who had stopped inching and who were now pointing their fingers, as well as their weapons, at them?

"Maybe we should."

North turned toward the advancing kids, who were shouting, "What about us? We elected you to take care of *us*."

"And you guys, don't worry," he said. "Because Governor Belt just told me that he's going to give each of you the same exact things that he gave to Winchell in the form of endowments and perks."

The kids' reaction?

"Will we get yachts?"

North's retort?

"Oh, you'll get yachts. Unless the Governor changes his mind. But I don't think he'll do that. Hey, do you really think that he wants to become known as the reversible Belt?"

The kids' reaction?

"Reversible belt?" Followed by laughter.

The folks' reaction?

Pretty much the same.

Mom's reaction?

"North tells a good joke."

Dad's reaction?

"He gets it from my side of the family."

Yes! But did North stop here? No!

"Governor Belt, ladies and gentlemen. Come over here, Governor."

"You'll never get away with this, North."

"Oh?"

"North, I can't possibly give everybody everything they want."

"Tell that to *them*," said North, referring to the thousands of kids and folks who had stopped laughing and were now staring at Arthur Belt, anxiously awaiting what he had to say.

And though he didn't have a stopwatch on him, North was willing to bet anything that when Arthur Belt looked out at that crowd, he set a new speed record for having blood drain from a governor's face. But, once again, the ever glib, always eloquent Arthur Belt rose to the occasion by clearing his throat and proclaiming, "It's going to be great. Everything's going to be just fine."

Yes! The crowd went nuts! North grabbed the microphone again.

"Good speech, Governor. And a nice plaid sports jacket, by the way. Which reminds me, Governor. Do you know the difference between a bathroom and a red carnation in someone's lapel?"

"No, I don't."

"Hey, Winchell, I'd be careful when you're around this guy if I were you."

Laughing. Thousands and thousands of people were now laughing.

"Come here and take a bow, Winchell. You're such a good sport. As a matter of fact, all of you—Winchell, Surgeon General Large, Chief Justice Buckle, Governor Belt . . ."

Applauding. Cheering. Thousands and thousands of people applauding and cheering.

"You know," said North into the mike, his hands

over his head in an attempt to get everyone to stop applauding and cheering, "you know, when you have a situation like this where thousands are in a stadium, laughing and feeling good that a misunderstanding has been cleared up, it's often the people *behind* the scenes that don't get the credit that they really deserve. Winchell, Governor Belt, Surgeon General Large, Chief Justice Buckle—thank you. Thank you for everything that you're going to do to satisfy *everyone*."

More applauding. More cheering. During which a bowing Winchell looked at North and said under his breath, "Some friend *you* turned out to be."

"Ladies and gentlemen," North yelled into the mike. "Winchell has just told me that everyone is invited back to his estate, where all the kids and all the folks will be able to sit down and discuss everything over cake and coffee. Isn't that nice?"

Everyone's reaction?

"Yes!"

A voice from the crowd yelled out, "Hey, North, what about *your* folks?"

"Oh, don't worry. *I'll* take care of them," said North, nodding his head and chuckling. And while no one really knew what that nod and chuckle and inflection were supposed to mean, everyone laughed anyway. Yes, North had this audience in the palm of his hand and they would have laughed at anything he said at this point. But Joey Fingers had taught him how important it was to know when to get off, so he looked at the bandleader and said, "Maestro, if you will . . ." and then waited for the music to begin. But since the band had never worked with North before, everyone just started playing whatever song each one felt like playing, and the happy crowd started singing whatever song each one of them felt like singing as they closed in on the gallows, hoisted Winchell, Governor Belt, Chief Justice Buckle, and Surgeon General Large onto their shoulders, and made their way out of the stadium.

And then there were three. North, Mom, and Dad. Alone in an empty North Memorial Stadium.

North was a little sad. Joey Fingers would've been proud of him had he lived to see North's performance. But then again, he would never have met Joey Fingers in the first place had he not left the folks who were still bound on the gallows beside him. North wondered if he should now thank them for having been as obnoxious as they used to be because it had given him the opportunity to have met Joey. But then again, who ever heard of thanking someone for being obnoxious? Oh, it was all so confusing.

"Son?"

"Yes, Dad?"

"That was quite a little show you put on."

"Thanks, Dad."

"We're proud of you, North."

"Thanks, Mom."

"Son?"

"Yes, Dad?"

"Didn't you get your sense of humor from me?"

"Son?"

"Yes, Mom?"

"I'm funnier than Dad, aren't I?"

"He got it from me."

"He did not, he got it from me."

"From me."

"From me."

"Mom!"

"From me."

"From me."

"Dad!"

"From me."

"Mom! Dad!"

"Yes, North."

"Watch it!"

"We were just kidding, North."

"North?"

"Yes, Dad?"

"Let's go home, son."

"No."

And with that, North jumped off the platform, untethered the Amish horse, went back up to the gallows, untied the ropes that bound his folks to those wooden stakes, kissed them both on their cheeks, escorted them into the Amish buggy, and slowly drove them out of the empty stadium to the department store—to his secret spot—where the three of them could sit and talk privately and maturely.

Hey, North wanted to find out if his folks *really* learned something from all this.

ALAN ZWEIBEL was born in Brooklyn, New York, in
1950. He grew up on Long Island and graduated from the
University of Buffalo. After being rejected by virtually
every law school in the English-speaking world, he started
writing gags and comedy routines for over one hundred
stand-up comics. In 1975 he became a writer for the original *Saturday Night Live*. He has won three Emmys and
two Writers Guild Awards. On Broadway, he was a contrib-
utor to *Gilda Live!* His fiction has appeared in *The Atlantic*.
Alan Zweibel lives in New York City with his wife, Robin,
and son, Adam, who'll be disowned if he ever pulls a stunt
like North did.